The God of Glass

The Peter Redgrove Library

Other Peter Redgrove books available from Stride:

The Peter Redgrove Library:
1. *In the Country of the Skin*
2. *The Terrors of Dr. Treviles**
3. *The Glass Cottage**
4. *The God of Glass*
5. *The Sleep of the Great Hypnotist*
6. *The Beekeepers*
7. *The Facilitators*
8. *The Colour of Radio: Essays and Interviews*
[*with Penelope Shuttle]

The Laborators
Abyssophone
Orchard End
What the Black Mirror Saw
Sheen
A Singer for the Silver Goddess

A Curious Architecture [contributor]
Earth Ascending [contributor]

i.m. Peter Redgrove:
Full of Star's Dreaming: Peter Redgrove 1932-2003

The God of Glass

A Morality

Peter Redgrove

The God of Glass
This edition 2006
© Peter Redgrove, 1979
© The Estate of Peter Redgrove, 2006
Introduction © Jay Ramsay, 2006

All rights reserved

ISBN 1-905024-11-8

Cover design by Neil Annat
Cover photos © Alistair Fitchett
Used with kind permission of the artist

The Peter Redgrove Library
is published by
Stride Publications
4b Tremayne Close
Devoran
Cornwall TR3 6QE
England

www.stridebooks.co.uk

Thanks

The Peter Redgrove Library is grateful to the following subscribers who have helped make the publication of these titles possible:

Cliff Ashcroft
Andrew Bailey
Martin Bax
Hazel Carruthers
Philip Fried
Mark Goodwin & Nikki Clayton
David Grubb
Michael Longley
Adrian & Celia Mitchell
Brian Louis Pearce
Malcolm Ritchie
Geoff Sutton & Bernard Gilhooly
Leonie Whitton & David Westby

to the following for help, encouragement and support in other ways:

Tony Frazer
Neil Roberts
Penelope Shuttle
the late Philip Hobsbaum

and to Arts Council England, South West for financial support.

Introduction

Geoffrey Glass: innocent or guilty? And by whose judgement? Whose morality? Whose religion?

This is the drama of *The God of Glass*, which Peter Redgrove — who was so much a poet first and foremost — brings definite novelistic skills to, largely of suspense in the story itself, and also in how we and others see its main character, this elusive priestly African with his oddly Anglicized name, a stranger in a small rural Devon village in the midst of all kinds of strange goings on.

Redgrove handles this with skill as well as subtlety: Glass seems by turns 'guilty as hell' and more innocent than ordinary morality can sanction. The suspense, which holds the narrative and keeps it tightly sprung throughout what is essentially a novella, is in this slippery alternation. Here he is in conversation with Dr Pocket, as the doctor refers to one of the young female victims:

> 'But first her madness — or whatever it was — made a kind of joke of it.'
>
> 'A joke? What did she say?'
>
> 'It was a phrase, repeated once or twice, like a little chant. She said: "Missed a glass, missed a glass, missed a glass!" And that's your name — Mr. Glass! Nothing in it but coincidence, I suppose, but strange all the same'.
>
> 'One, two and three — missed a glass; one, two — missed a glass.'
>
> 'What?'
>
> 'It's from a Father Brown story. G.K. Chesterton. Called *The Absence of Mr Glass* . . .'

— as we breathe out again, momentarily at least. And throughout, the biblical phrase from Corinthians 'we see through a glass darkly, and then face to face' is an unspoken subtext for the whole narrative, with its root story carried by the rather marvellous Sylvia Pendennis (the pun is on Thackeray), who manages to double as a cool barrister and a reincarnated witch.

She is also a powerful female mouthpiece, of course, for Peter's own timely (if not prophetic) preoccupation with feminism and paganism, anticipating the 1980s with its resurgence through Wicca and Druidry, among various groups and individuals like Starhawk, here and in America. Peter's counterpoint is a bloodless and hypocritical Christianity, or what we should call 'Churchianity' since it has little to do with what Jesus actually taught. This is what is travestied here; at the same time Redgrove is aware of the savagery of the opposite polarity, repressed as it also is, which Glass mysteriously mediates and potentially transforms (for 'glass' here we can also read 'alembic' or alchemical vessel).

This is one of the central tensions of Redgrove's work which he explores subsequently (and arrestingly) in *The Black Goddess & The Sixth Sense*, and in a poem like 'The Idea of Entropy at Maenporth Beach', where light and dark, white and black, are seriously played with as the woman in the white bridal dress 'slips back into the muck' of the mud ooze. Redgrove's own emphasis is on physicalizing spirituality as a way of also expressing its complexity which he sees reflected in the created world, something that simplistic morality (with all its lack of creativity) cannot grasp or celebrate. His own religion is broadly pantheistic then, which we may also come to see as its limitation; because as real as the spiritual world undoubtedly is, it is ultimately non-physical.

The God Of Glass, then, addresses what is a central concern for its author (and his wife and co-worker, Penelope Shuttle) which is also a political and karmic issue: the subjugation and repression of the feminine. Whether it is simply a vehicle for this moral debate re-enacted through fiction is really up to each reader to decide; and without giving away the demise of the story, I would say you have to keep turning the pages to really find out.

Jay Ramsay

Acknowledgements

The God of Glass originated in Peter Redgrove's play of the same title, which was commissioned by the BBC in 1974, and was first broadcast on Radio 3 on 31 July 1977, with Brian Miller producing, and Yemi Ajibade in the title-role and Anna Cropper as Sylvia Pendennis. The play won the Imperial Tobacco Award for Radio Drama (Original Single Play) in 1978. The quotation on page 31 is from *The Symphony of Life* by Donald Hatch Andrews (Unity Books, 1966). The verses in the last chapter are freely adapted from Max Pulver's translation of the so-called 'Hymn of Jesus' from the New Testament Apocryphal Acts of St John, which appears in Max Pulver, 'Jesus' Round Dance and Crucifixion According to the Acts of St. John', in *The Mysteries: Papers from the Eranos Yearbooks, vol. 2,* ed. Joseph Campbell, trans. Ralph Manheim, Bollingen Series XXX. Copyright © 1955 by Princeton University Press. Material adapted by permission of Princeton University Press and of Routledge & Kegan Paul.

Prologue

The judge had a slight cold. Every now and again he raised a lace-trimmed handkerchief to his nose to dab it: his voice was hoarse; he had several times snapped at counsel. He had replaced his big, full-bottomed wig in which he had made his entrance with a short curly one under which his coal-black hair made a startling contrast. The red of his robe and the snowy white of his neck-linen, and his ermine sleeve with the animal's black streaks showing, made him a figure of red, white and black that had bound Geoffrey Glass in a spell ever since the trial had started. As the guilty man, black Glass was fenced away from the rest of the crowded courtroom in a little kiosk with a policeman, looking very vulnerable without his helmet, on a chair to his side and slightly behind him. He had this vantage-point, raised like a judge's dais, so that the main actors in this drama, or dancers in this dance, were all at the same level; for the jury-box, full of eleven good men and true and one grey-haired woman, was raised too, and stood directly opposite the dock, which was on the judge's right.

To Glass it was like a dance, a slow dance, with enthroned principal dancers, and most of the work done by scurrying figures. The faces did not matter. It was the bodies that mattered, and the bodies of this cold people of a cold climate were masked, so that they expressed only their masks' function. Where Glass came from, masks were no concealment, since the body itself was usually only lightly clothed. In this country, the faces were like gravestones, unaltering, unyielding, and the bodies wore uniforms and robes of function.

'Gentlemen of the jury, have you reached a verdict?'

'We have, my lord.'

'What is your verdict?'

Glass was conscious of no tension. He was held in the dance. The great red, white and black-marked mask of the judge rustled and bowed as it spoke, and dabbed its featureless face with a frippery cloth. The drab juryman standing in the box opposite to deliver his verdict did so like the ghost of an African, with a dead-white face.

'Guilty, my lord.'

Glass saw his hands shaking. Why should they not shake? They had done a terrible thing. The great carcass of robes, fatty white, dried-blood black, meaty red, turned his bony face that sniffled, and boomed:

'The prisoner will stand.'

Glass found the courtroom shrinking, becoming remote. It had descended a little. He was on his feet. The body of his guilt had brought him to his feet, and his mind was detached and clear.

'Geoffrey Glass, you have been convicted of an abominable crime, for which I can find no excuse in circumstance or nature. The defence has brought forward witnesses to testify to your character and behaviour since you entered this country not many years ago, and we have heard the evidence of psychiatrists who have spoken of the strange savagery of your crime, and the motives that might or might not lie behind it. Indeed, in all the annals of criminal history, I have never heard of one man doing such a terrible thing to another. Moreover, you are a stranger to our country. You have refused interviews with these doctors, and observation by them; you have appeared throughout your remand in prison and your trial very calm and unmoved; I might almost say callous. I have tried to make every allowance for you, such allowance as might apply to the fact of your negro colour, and your belonging to an ethnic minority, whose behaviour and manners diverge from our own. The law in such cases as yours allows me to be lenient, to treat even such a savage killing as a form of manslaughter. But in your case I now believe it to be a deliberate and savage murder. Have you anything to say before sentence is passed?'

Glass looked down at his hands, which were still working. He spoke from the body of his guilt.

'Speak up, prisoner, you must speak up.'

The body of his guilt within was coloured like the judge in exposed rib-colours, in black bile colours, in fiery meat colours. It was his own judge, inside him, bearing the colours of what is within the skin of every man.

'I am guilty, my lord. Guilty as — hell.'

'As hell? Your language is as immoderate as your crime, but I am enabled to punish you only for the latter,' said the judge, wiping his nose once again, and tucking that fussy little handkerchief into his great ermine sleeve. There was an usher standing by the judge's elbow carrying a little red cushion, and on the cushion was folded the black square of linen, the black cap, that the judge had to wear when he was sentencing people to death. The usher stepped forward, but the judge motioned him back. A sigh went over the courtroom.

'It only remains for me to pass sentence. You shall be taken from hence to a safe place, and there imprisoned — for the term of your natural life.'

Glass felt the words enter his ears like some worm or spirit with the raspy feet of a sniff. The worms entered the mouth of the second judge that sat enthroned in the centre of Glass's black courtroom inside his black head and dropped from it again like maggots that were printed letters spelling out his sentence repeatedly. The white letters seemed to writhe over all his black skin. The body of his guilt spoke from Glass's mouth.

'Thank you, my lord . . .'

But his voice came out in a strange roar and the policeman at his back stepped forward.

The judge looked startled.

'Thank you, my lord . . .'

And then Glass paused. The body of his guilt was a dead man, after all, and now the dead man had forgotten his words.

'Thank you, my lord . . .'

All the faces in the courtroom were turned toward him, and the boom of his voice still echoed. The judge rustled impatiently and was turning away again when Glass spoke to his judge for the last time, his voice cracking and howling like an animal's voice.

'Thank you, my lord — for giving me Life.'

The policeman in the dock gripped his arm and turned him unresisting towards the cells.

Chapter 1

It was a high, still day. The sky was unusually steep, and the icy water-houses of cloud floated high above the warm little village. The furrowed fields were as smooth as corduroy with the spring shoots. The trees bounced with neat white buds, each wrapped crosswise, snug as the robe of a Buddhist priest, imitating the lotus. These lamps lightened the trees even now, before the leaves had properly sprung.

The little stone cottage nestled in the bend of the valley stream that foamed with the spring spate; and there was a yeasty smell of it in the air. This stream was streaked with the currents of its speed, and glittered in the sunlight like electricity. It was a neat stone cottage, very foursquare, with two windows up and down each side of a front door wreathed in budding creeper. The valley rose behind it, keeping it snug on a shelf of rock. To one side there was a garage, and to the other a clear grassy space with a beehive close up to the stone wall to catch its heat. The bees would be laying now, filling their dome with new workers, whose wings would bring the nectar and pollen on which the hive, a complete organism of winged cells, would feed, and upon which, as stored honey, it had fed its diminished numbers all winter. As the spring moved into summer, so the hum of the power of the hive would increase, until it would dominate like an under-bass the little glade. These bees would work the whole valley, combining its scents and sweetness into its own body, that hummed gently like the *Om* of an Indian saint.

In the quiet sun, there was only the sound of the water streaking down from the hills, the gentle bees, and spurts of liquid birdsong from the tall trees and the steep blue sky.

Then the cottage screamed! And screamed again. A pane of glass burst from the lefthand upstairs window, and clattered down on the stone pathway beneath. Through the empty wooden frame the screams poured and there were sobs too, and laughter and terrible distressed low speech. Then a lull, and in that lull men's voices chanting quickly and desperately, and then, as though the little stream outside had suddenly flooded swollen down from the hills, a terrible wall of sound like voices welded together and rushing forwards.

'MY BROTHER MY BROTHER TWENTY YEARS KILLED AND NOT DEAD YET IN THE WORLD OF POLLEN FOUNTAINS AH AH AAH WHO THE GLASS APPLE WITH LIGHT SHINING IN THE CORE THE SHADOWS TROOP OH TAKE ME TAKE ME BURY ME I CANNOT SEE ENOUGH I SEE TOO MUCH EACH HOLLY LEAF IS HAND-SEWN AND HAND PAINTED THE PIPS LIKE GLASS IN WHICH THE EMBRYOS SHOW I HAVE SUCCEEDED THEY CRY OUT   AAAAH LET US HUM   YOU HAVE   SUCCEEDED? YOU NO LONGER EXIST THEY SHOUT   THE SILK LUNGS STRETCHED LIKE SAILS WITH THE WIND   LISTEN TO IT LISTEN TO IT   A BARREL OF SWEAT SHAKEN OFF THE GREAT TREE I PULL OUT A GLUE GHOST FROM ME FROM HERE A PUNGENT BROWN GHOST THE TREES WILL NOT KEEP STILL KEEP STILL STILL'

In the cottage bedroom with its bright flowery wallpaper two clergymen with their books and their long black robes and sweating faces are chanting to a bed with vomit-splashed pillows. On the bed a child lies asleep.

'O God, the protector and creator of men, look kindly upon Mary Ann Rose, your servant, and O Lord banish from her the power that has lodged in her . . .'

The little girl in the bed stirs gently, and smiles in her sleep. Suddenly her eyes open wide and her face swells with the stretching of her mouth and the calling out of her swollen throat:

'I THINK YOU ARE GOING TO WRITE ON ME WITH CONCEALED KNIVES   AAAAAAH THE HAUNTED CARVING KNIFE THE SPIRIT LIVES IN THE BLADE IT LOOKS JUST LIKE A MAN ABOUT TO DIE ON THE BRINK OF IT ON THE KNIFE EDGE I PLACE THE POINT IN YOUR THROAT HOLLOW I'D LIKE TO LOOK AT THE IMAGE ON THE BLADE MEAT WITH ITS CLOTHES ON MEAT WITH ITS CLOTHES ON   SHALL I DRIVE THE POINT HOME'

The two tall men, still reading their books, cannot make themselves heard above this bellow, and a stinking wind blows out of that mouth as the face of it tugs to and fro on the retaining straps.

'Dispossess for evermore the deceitful treachery of these powers, banish from her these demons. Strengthen your servant Mary Ann Rose with your glory and lend her stamina in mind and body . . .'

Then the elder of the two clergymen takes up a wooden crucifix and the two in unison call out through the torrent of sounds pouring from the face on the bed, and its voice rises in pitch and strength as though with contemptuous power and versatility to sweep them away, like the thunder of a storm.

'In the Name of Jesus Christ Our Lord In the Name of Jesus Christ our Lord In the Name of Jesus Christ Our Lord.'

The older priest's hands, knotted about the shaft of his crucifix, twist in an odd way, and the wood snaps. There is a defiant bellow of laughter from the tossing face on the bed. Then silence. The silence goes on, and the echoes of that terrible voice die away. The sound of the rushing stream outside comes into the room, faintly and gratefully. The two men relax, and look down into the stained and rumpled bed, where a child of about ten is sleeping. As they look at her, her eyes slowly open, the lashes brushing together. The men flinch a little, in case the demon they are exorcising is still behind the mask of the little girl. The eyes smile at them. The mouth smiles. It is terribly parched and encrusted.

'Father, can I have some water? I'm terribly thirsty. Can I have a glass of water please, Father?'

The elder priest steps closer to the bed. The restraining straps and webbing hold the body secure, but the one arm has worked free. The brass pillars of the bed gleam, except where a splash of vomit hangs on the bedrail and stains the wallpaper behind. The younger man is clearly as exhausted as his companion but moves quickly round the bed and restrains him.

'In God's name, Father, finish the exorcism! This may still be the demon. We must finish the ritual.'

The old man looks down on the child, and sighs, and smiles. Mary Ann Rose smiles back, and lifts her hand toward him. Smiling, he reaches behind him for the bottle of water on the windowsill and while his companion reads from his book, sprinkles holy water on the child and on the bed.

'Give Grace by your name, O Lord, that this terror who is the prince of wicked serpents may now glide in terror himself from this child, the temple of thy spirit.

And now there is nothing but a stretching mouth on the bed out of which blackness and foulness the words fly and the laughter

'WORDS EH FATHER YOU CAN LOVE CAN YOU YOU DONT LOVE YOU WOULD NOT LOVE THIS CHILD WITH THAT WITHERED TASSEL HANGING BENEATH YOUR KNEES UNDER YOUR FROCK OH LET ME NIP IT OFF WITH MOUTH MOUTH PRIEST AND SUCK YOUR BLOOD FROM YOUR WITHERED COCK THAT WOULD BE ALL YOU COULD GIVE FROM THAT BLOOD FROM THE SEVERANCE LET ME HAVE THAT LITTLE MUSHROOM MORSEL AND SWALLOW IT SINCE YOU HAVE NO USE FOR IT AND I WILL TURN IT TO TURDS LIKE ALL TURNS TO TURDS'

and now from that mouth something brown is inching and with another smile that is like a smile round a big fat cigar and a foul smell the face shits from its mouth and the steaming caterpillar crawls down its chin and on to the pillow as the priests shaking and sick call out and the face on the bed rolls itself from side to side pasting brown over its right profile.

'In the Name of Jesus Christ Our Lord In the Name of Jesus Christ Our Lord In the Name of Jesus Christ Our Lord' and the holy water glitters flying through the air.

The child-demon continues to bellow but now it lows like a cow and as the holy water strikes the parched skin there are cries of pain also. The priests' eyes are tight shut to keep steadfast against the noise and so they cannot see the violent tossing of the besmeared head with the howling mouth trying to avoid the holy water that the older man shakes over her as he chants. Then once again there is silence.

The sound of the stream fills the stillness. The two men carefully open their eyes and look down on the bed, where a sleeping child with a pathetically smeared face lies. She looks up and smiles.

'Father, I'm so thirsty. Please give me a glass of water to drink, Father . . .'

'Father, take care! If it is the demon it will have the strength of ten. Better to repeat the exorcism.'

'The child's lips are parched, John, so parched. . .' And he takes a jug and a glass from a shelf by the window, and pours a glass of water. First he blesses it.

'Blessed creature of water, succour this child.'

Then he comes forward and takes the child's head in his hand and puts the water to her lips.

'There, Mary Ann, let me help you . . . you've not been well, dear.'

She drinks, and looks at him gratefully. But the younger priest catches a sidelong glint in her eye. Before he can do anything, the demon is back, howling from a square letter-box mouth, and she has the old priest in a grip with one arm round his neck. With the other hand she snatches the glass from him, and smashes it on the metal of the bedstead. It is a jagged weapon, like the broken bottle of a pub brawl, and she slashes at the priest's throat with it, bringing his neck where the pulse beats down on to her razor-edged glass despite his struggles and screams which now replace the howling that she has ceased to make. She works silently; it is the priest's howls that plunge again and again rhythmically from his pillar-box mouth, and the blood leaps out of this second mouth that she saws in his throat like the colour of the pillar-box painting them both. First a sheet of purple dashes like spray mixed with the foam of his calling-out that is taking this second route from his lungs, then as her freshly-minted blade bites deeper, the carotid below the ear is severed in a great grin and the blood begins leaping and boxing like hares of blood playing on a meadow of blood, as the bright crimson spreads over the sheets and the priest's black robes, clotting the face and hair of the demon: it binds them together, priest and girl, in one flow of colour. The priest kicks feebly and the younger man kneels by the bed, retching. The demon with a face of blood leans an elbow on the priest-carcass and licks her lips preparatory to speaking.

'He missed a glass, didn't he, he missed that trick, dear John, and now if he could talk he has two mouths to talk through. In church, on Sunday, which he will now only once more attend, (and that will be his own funeral) . . .'

The blood-and-black corpse face-downwards on the bed jerks with a tremor, as if it were a black umbrella shaking itself a little free from a blood-rain.

'That was nice, a little spasm, did he feel it or has his soul flown. They say that dead people ejaculate — is it true?'

She reaches down and heaves the body over so that she can unzip the fly and reach in. She feels around, and brings out a little white mucus, which she sniffs and tastes.

'Ah well it is. He was a blessed soul then, with a great love of death. Death embraced him, and he came into her embrace. But that was me wasn't it? Then I should have his child — let me try.'

Now she reaches down again for more of the mucus, and having secured some on her forefinger carefully lifts the skirt of her nightdress and plunges her forefinger into her small genitals, rubbing and gasping. A tremor runs over her like the spasm of the vicar's corpse.

'Aaah, that was lovely, wasn't it, lover?'

She speaks now crooningly to the dead man. There is blood on her finger, which she wiggles at herself, and then sucks off again. She puts her finger into the priest's open throat, that is still bleeding sluggishly, and tastes it.

'Missed the glass! Not at all careful, my laddo. And now you have got me with child, though I see I am bleeding too. All that excitement, no doubt when my bridegroom took me, the virgin of the voices!'

The cultivated voice she has been speaking in is succeeded by a great bellow like a bull, and then a miaow of particular length and sinuousness like a cat and a tom stalking each other: indeed, it seems a double cry, as though she were making the sounds of both animals at once. Then the bull-cry shakes the room once again.

'Then, were he the walking dead, he would climb up into coward's castle — the pulpit, dear frightened John — and preach two sermons at once: the sermon of the priest, and the undersermon of the priest's body. Look, John!'

While she has been talking, the booming of the bull's voice has been continuing, but from slightly another direction. Its source is difficult to ascertain, but now she lifts her skirt and John can see that her vulva is stretched and pouting and it is from this that the bellowing sound comes, muted, and a smell that makes his head reel again. He cannot swear to all these happenings, he cannot tell that they are true, only that he sees them; and now the greatest horror of all, because the cultivated discourse of the lecturing voice continues, and it seems to him that it comes from the vulva of the little girl, stained with the blood of her period and the blood of the priest, within it lodged the living semen of the dead man, even now spreading into her womb. It seems to him that the lips, the labia of the girl, are writhing and framing these words.

'My undersermon, John. How would you like me to write these words along your stiff, strong priest-love, John? This is how love talks, my lover. Come to me. Join with us here on this bed, and take your turn, dearie. You must listen, Johnnie, your ears have been closed. This is what it is like if you leave us unlistened to too long.' A dreadful gust of a smell that the Rev. John later describes as onions fried with shit blows from that little girl's place. 'John, you should have listened before, you would not see me like this. I loved you, John, and now I must leave you. This is the other side of what you preached, Reverend, and what you have made it.' That terrible smell again. The little girl pulls down the skirt of her nightdress, and speaks from her demon-head.

'You have made me speak in two voices, when I wished to talk in one voice. Listen.' It is the sound of the hive down in the garden coming from her mouth. Suddenly he is striking at the air, which, he said later, seemed full of bees swarming. He was panic-stricken because he thought that he would get stung and swell up like a drowned man. He must have run a few steps because when he was next conscious he found himself with her arm, that felt like a steel band, holding him round the neck, he looked into the blood-flecked eyes of the demon, the black pupils contracted to a point in the oyster-grey eyes, and the stench from the bloody mouth nearly robbing him of consciousness again. The light flittered off the stained, jagged toothglass that she had killed his friend with. The front of his body was lying up against the corpse, and some time must have passed, since he felt that it was cold, and a cold serum from the blood was penetrating his clothes.

'John, you must listen. My name is Legion, because you have shattered my reflection.' The little girl's body that the demon had lodged in was clearly exhausted. As it took breath he could hear a wheezing from the lungs, though the eyes gleamed with joy. In that wheezing he could also hear the voices of many animals. 'I cannot see myself except in you, and your fear and your religion have taken me to pieces. But I have a legion of voices to talk with. Did you like the way I outflanked you with the bees? Names and amens didn't help, did they? Look at all the blood, speaking in its many tongues.' John believes he saw in the dark red blotches and clots an army of banners passing, locked trains from which people are calling. 'Blood like a stuck pig. Red and greasy. You grease us, priest, but do you ease us?' The demon now seems to be losing control through exhaustion, her head feebly wobbles from side to side as she chants rhythmically, and once again her voice rises to a bellow passing to a shriek of many voices rising and rising beyond the limits of audibility: JESUS ESUS JESUS ESUS JESUS ESUS JESUS ESUS JEEZ JEEEEEEEEEZE JESUS JESUS JESUS.' The name becomes an automatism that the being cannot free itself from though it is struggling to control it, and the corners of the mouth visibly tear and bleed as John watches, held in the vice of the crook of her forearm.

'Your vicar could tell all now, but all he does from his undermouth is to bleed. Listen to me talk from all my mouths.' Another crescendo of voices begins, but to John the voices start mildly, and strangely, since the pillar-box mouth is clammed shut, and he can see, close up as he is, the little tearducts in the lower eyelids talking with tiny voices, and he stares into the pupils of those grey eyes and suddenly the pin-point blackness enlarges and slits, and begins talking like grey lips, and then the black clotted nostrils twitch and move together and part and begin talking, and from the sides of the head under the matted hair the small voices of the ears join the chorus, then the mouth opens and a little voice comes from that, and then from behind his head he can hear the three voices starting up from under the skirt.

'My mouth, my two mouths, my three mouths, my four mouths,' say all the voices as they are enumerated, 'my five mouths, my six mouths, my seven mouths, my eight mouths, my mouths to the count of a sacred twelve mouths. Listen to my ears singing! Listen to the three pigs that grunt between my legs. Oh poor clergyman-lovers, missed a glass, missed a glass, missed a glass . . .' Twirling the jagged edges in front of his eyes . . . 'How cutting!' Shrieks of laughter from all mouths at this witticism. 'But tell me this, John old man, and listen to this, though they call me the father of lies I undertake now to tell you the utter truth, upon my age I swear, upon my throne at the right hand of God, this I swear and this is true, and if you cannot see this you deserve to die the death that I have reserved for your kind. Here is the truth: you are closer to Deity than you have ever been. If you can understand my voices, then you will draw near to me. If you cannot, then they will take you to pieces. Like this, John, like this.' And the jagged glass saws near his eyes, and then towards the face of the child, as the demon-body saws at its own little neck and the warm blood flies again into his face with the light touch of love bringing with it blackness and unconsciousness as the iron arm of the little girl of ten released itself from around his neck and he slumps over the corpse of his dead friend on the putrid carpet.

Chapter 2

'Man that is born of a woman hath but a short time to live, and is full of misery. He cometh up, and is down, like a flower. . .'

John Cuttance was reading the burial service over the mutilated body of his friend, having read it already over the terribly torn corpse of the little girl they had tried to exorcise together, Mary Ann Rose Trevelyan. He had had some doubts whether he should not refuse Christian burial to the girl, after the events he had witnessed, and after what he called alternately in his mind 'suicide' and 'murder by demon or demons unknown'.

He had woken from his faint in the light of the moon, and it was a blessing, since it concealed rather than revealed the sight of the bed. Through the window had come the soothing sound of the stream, and a scent of honeysuckle from the night breeze. He lay there for a moment and then suddenly recalled where he was. He writhed with horror. With an effort he made an act of recollection and uttered a short prayer. Then, moving carefully so as to avoid touching anything there, he got up and hurried downstairs. He got out of the dark cottage safely, and ran through the night to the doctor's house. There had to be some hushing-up. Fortunately for them, Mrs Trevelyan had taken her little girl straight to the doctor when the strange utterances and incontinences had begun to appear, and the GP was thankful he had sent them to an eminent psychiatrist in Plymouth. John arrived wild-eyed and blood-stained in the doctor's house, but before he would rest he persuaded Dr Pocket to ring up the consultant and prime him before the police came.

John would never forget his first sight of Mrs Trevelyan after the exorcism and its terrible outcome. Dr Pocket had prescribed whisky and a tranquilliser. John had swallowed the one and was sipping the other when Mrs Trevelyan entered. She had been sent to her sister while the exorcism was in progress. She came in. She wore her macintosh, though it was not raining, quite a butch garment for a middle-aged woman, with many buckles and straps. Incongruously she wore also a large light-yellow straw hat. She came silently into the room and caught sight of John sipping his whisky under the light of the desk lamp, which must have shown the darker stains on his dark garment. John looked up to see swimming in front of his gaze what seemed to him a large yellow moon with reddened mouth and false eyelashes. Mrs Trevelyan had guessed that something terrible had happened, and her skin blanched the colour of the straw of her hat. John got up and guided her to a chair.

'Forasmuch as it had pleased Almighty God of his great mercy to take unto himself the soul of our dear Brother in Christ, Alexander Chesney Bodkin here departed . . .'

His kind vicar and mentor Alex Bodkin dead! Not a wise man; certainly in the grip of a compulsion to force the dark energies of this girl's possession back where they came from; but a kindly one, and an enthusiastic one. He had long been interested, John knew, in exorcism as an approach to mental illness proper for a man of the Church, and there had been trouble of this kind once before. Once he had dabbled in psychiatry, out of pure friendship with a noted doctor, Gregory Treviles, and there had been another suicide. Nor had he on this second occasion seen fit to consult his bishop.

'We therefore commit their bodies to the ground; earth to earth, ashes to ashes, dust to dust . . .'

The daffodils blazed on the slopes that led to the sunken graveyard beneath which the valley stream ran. Soon, John thought, both Alex and Mary Ann would be pollen blowing from the luminous trumpets of such flowers, and they would begin their long climb through the foodchains until they had human speech again. What if they retained memory of their existence in other forms: as the pollen growing up from the molecule in the tight bud of the daffodil, drawing up its nourishment from the hell of graveyard juices, lying in the bright tents of the flower among the flowers' scents of passion, spooned out by the bees' legs and taken for a flight to the humming hive, and there laid down as food for the tiny bee-maggots, or to be spread on the bread and butter of another country clergyman, or that of Mrs Trevelyan, eating up the honey from her own daughter's grave?

Ah, he had never had these thoughts before; he was still shaken by the voice of the demon that had leered into his face and told him he was nearer at that moment to Deity than ever before in this life. Would Jesus be his guide through the staircases of the atom? Not the Jesus he knew, the always-human. It would be somebody as powerful as the spirit that possessed that little girl, who had changed so before his eyes. And would he in these natural changes be lost like the soul of the little girl he was now burying in the rich soil?

Dr Pocket was no less shaken by the outcome of the vicar's experiments, and indeed felt heavy responsibility for them. In a small community like this, in Petroc, just a couple of valleys, really, running down to a little hardly-used port, it was so easy to magnify the abilities of the people who administered the community, and whom one knew so well that they had become identified with their functions. He used to say to himself that he had never lost a patient, except to old age: oh, that was true enough, but only because so many of the young people were moving away from the area when they grew up, and the babies and pregnancies were pretty healthy.

So he became here, because of a social accident, the beloved physician, esteemed and over-estimated. That, he supposed, turned Bodkin into God! He never thought to question the vicar's desire to exorcise the child, when it seemed that it was dangerous to prescribe stronger drugs for her spasms, and the psychiatrist, a friend of Treviles' in Plymouth, had assured him that this was merely a 'hyperkinetic disorder of adolescence' that the passing of adolescence would cure. Pocket was coroner too, and the police inspector was his half-brother. This meant the inquest could be held without interesting the local paper, whose office was at Plymouth, though if there were any more of these cases he doubted whether it could be kept quiet much longer.

Why should little, quiet, isolated Petroc so excite its daughters that they should undergo such experiences? Mary Ann Rose was the third death, and the worst of the three. Well, yes, he *had* lost patients, then, but only in the last eighteen months, after thirty years of practice. The first case he was able to put down as viral pneumonia. She died shouting with her lungs full of fluid, preternaturally feverish, almost burning the hand that touched her. He had taken a blood sample; he had wondered whether the girl's depressions before she fell acutely ill were due to that blood disease called brucellosis that people caught from infected milch-cows — he had dreamed of discovering a mutant strain. He had discussed the matter with the quiet black man who had settled in one of the ruined cottages high up on the little moor that started near where the valley trees stopped. It was strange to see a black man in this area. The locals were not at all sure about him; he was their first black. Twenty or even ten years ago he might have had trouble with the local lads after Saturday night in the pub, and he might have met with refusals in the village shops, but nowadays people were more curious and tolerant about the black folk from abroad who were making parts of London their own. Now even Petroc had a black man. It was not exactly that they were proud of him, but he added a certain modern flavour to their community, and they felt tolerant.

Geoffrey Glass first came to Dr Pocket's surgery because he had a swollen wrist from lifting and cementing the stones of his broken cottage into a home. He had turned suddenly and banged the hand against a sharp rock, and wondered whether he had a fracture. The joint merely required rest, and Pocket put it into a sling for him. Then they started talking. Glass had a reserve about him that was all the same a warmth, and the doctor immediately knew he had found a friend. Pocket cherished the idea of one day writing up his experiences as a coroner — drowning, mostly, off the fishing-boats — and he had kept his medico-legal knowledge brushed up. Glass turned out to have a surprising grasp of the field. When Pocket first went up to the half-finished cottage for a simple supper and a talk over some exquisite smoky liqueur whisky Glass kept, he was surprised to find the two rooms his friend lived in so bare. There were not the books he expected. There were two armchairs drawn up by the big cottage hearth, which still had the old baking ovens recessed in the brick — Glass kept a candle burning there during supper and afterwards so that the shadows playing with the rough walls of the little ovens continually fashioned strange, altering patterns — and a big table in the centre of the room for their supper. One curious feature the doctor did remark was another table, quite a small one, drawn up with a lamp on it against a large mirror bolted on to the wall. The table held this oil-lamp (since there was no electricity), and a small earthenware bowl of violets. A ladderback kitchen chair was placed with its seat tucked in underneath the table, so that there was room for the two to pass as they moved about the room from supper-table to armchairs. It was an ordinary table, but something about it impressed the doctor. It could have been used for writing: there was a small drawer under the top, perhaps for papers. He wondered what was remarkable about an ordinary kitchen table, with its grain showing and flowing through the top-surface. Then he realised what intrigued him. This surface was polished a deep honey-colour, and so carefully and so lustrously that one might have expected the effort to be expended on a much finer piece of furniture. As it was, the table they ate off was unpolished deal.

* * *

'Very, very shaken, I don't mind admitting it,' said Dr Pocket. He was walking through the valley with Glass, late in the day. The bark of the trees was soaked black with the spring rains, their new buds in the bare branches like a scattering of lights. He looked sideways at the black man, and wondered if he was a Yoruba. The Yoruba were one of the few notable African nations the Doctor had heard of, and he knew they were esteemed for their art and their tribal customs and their long history. He had heard that they were tall men, with heads held on straight necks, as Glass's was, proudly but not self-consciously, as a baby will first lift its head and look around at the world. He looked at Glass's great spread nose, with the cavernous nostrils that seemed capable of taking the forced draught of a furnace, and decided that Yoruba noses were straighter, and more conformable to the European idea of a handsome nose.

'Very, very shaken . . .'

'Were you in the bedroom when the killings occurred?' Glass's voice was a little flat, and oddly inflected. The doctor had not met many Africans. Glass stressed 'were' and the 'room' of 'bedroom' and left the rest of the sentence unstressed, as though that simple remark was waiting on its hind feet to spring forward.

'No, as the local GP I attended the case right from the beginning, and made a referral to a psychiatrist — I'm very glad I did, otherwise my position would have been uncomfortable. Then the parents called in the Church. They seemed to feel that my medical attitude was inappropriate. But I kept my eye on the case. I wish I had done more.'

'More?'

'I mean that I should have stayed throughout the exorcism, instead of riding my professional high horse. I might have been able to save both Mr Bodkin and the child. You do know, don't you, Mr Glass, that that — child — cut the throat of the officiating priest, and then her own throat? It all happened so fast. I prescribed tranquillisers, and she saw the psychiatrist. Then the voices got so strong, according to her parents, that it seemed beyond a medical phenomenon. I heard a little girl talking frantically, that was all. Then they said that objects were thrown about, and windows smashed. I saw convulsions, yes, but no more, and I relaxed the muscles with an injection. But I could not relax the soul, it seems. There was some energy come upon them that I do not understand! Then the two other girls. It is like a contagious epilepsy. And this morning, Glass —'

'This morning?' They had reached the bank of the rushing stream now, and stopped to inhale the bracing odour of the rushing water, and to listen to its sound. Through the thin-branched trees they could see a sprinkling of cottages, the beginning of the village.

'I am going to use the word "possession". These are cases of possession, though that is not a medical term. This morning I was called in to see the Pendennis girl. She has the same symptoms. And I found the curate there, that brave John Cuttance, who witnessed the killing of his vicar, and barely escaped with his own life. He had persuaded Mrs Pendennis to allow another exorcism. These people are my friends! I cannot call in the police. But they have slipped back to the Middle Ages. Another exorcism is in progress, Glass. Glass! That's a strange thing!'

'My name? It is a translation of a word that means "fixed

water", which in Africa we find only on the tops of mountains. The early traders used this word when they were selling us looking-glasses for the first time. They were ice, do you see, that could get warm in the sun, and reflect, and still not melt. My ancestors thought it an image of the constant thing within the flowing to and fro of our human life, that reproduces us in the same form generation after generation. It was at the same time an image of that which reproduces, and that which thinks and reflects about the generations. Thinking in these ways enables us to allow the images of truth to flow through our minds. A mirror reflects without holding on. We had beaten and polished metal to give us this symbol, but the white traders had obtained clearer glasses. They thought that we admired their mirrors for their prettiness. It was for their purity. We blacks were defenceless because we imagined that no person could make such images without possessing wisdom also. In that, we were sadly wrong. My great-great grandfather purchased and wore one of the white men's glasses, and danced them a greeting. He wore it on his chest so that they might see that he had taken them into his heart, and hoped that they would honour us by becoming part of our generations. The white men fortunately for us did not understand this compliment. They would have massacred us, instead of stealing our territories. We had exorcisms in our nation. I would like to see one of your exorcisms. I have never heard of anyone being killed in an exorcism. Perhaps your priests do not pay attention to what the demon is saying. Geoffrey means "God's peace".'

'I didn't mean your name, but the use that Mary Ann Rose made of it.' The doctor found that Geoffrey Glass — 'God's-peace fixed-water' — was staring straight at him, and he felt a bit small and colourless, like a little boy confronted with knowledgeable elders. Like a child, too, he saw Glass's features larger than life: the teeth were so white and the lips so large (and he felt his own lips, thinking that the sensation in them must be greatly magnified in those great sensoria of the black man) and the nostrils so cavernous that they seemed to be staring at him like the black pupils of the white eyes above, that showed a three-quarter disc over the lower eyelids like a dark brown sun rising over the black skyline in a white sky. And over the black skin, the natural oils made it seem to shine. He had skin like black glass, truly, like black glass, and the doctor giggled like a lost child deep inside.

'It was the use she made of it. I hope you don't mind this. It's rather — ghoulish, I'm afraid. According to the Rev. John almost the dead little girl's last words. Poor Mr Bodkin poured her some water. He was sorry for the little girl. Mary Ann broke the glass and used it like a razor, first on Bodkin, then on herself. But first her madness or whatever it was made a kind of joke of it.'

'A joke? What did she say?'

'It was a phrase, repeated once or twice, like a little chant. She said: "Missed a glass, missed a glass, missed a glass!" And that's your name — Mr Glass! Nothing in it but coincidence, I suppose, but strange all the same.'

'One, two and three — missed a glass; one, two — missed a glass.'

'What?'

'It's from a Father Brown story. G.K. Chesterton. Called *The Absence of Mr Glass.* A man is accused of killing one Mr Glass. He has been overheard talking to this Mr Glass behind locked doors. But when they break in there is no sign of this Mr Glass. So they accuse him of the murder of Glass. In reality this man is practising to be a juggler, using glass tumblers. Occasionally he drops one, and cries out "Missed a glass!" But there is no Mr Glass in that story and no corpse, and no murder. The police think there is, and by their misunderstanding create a murder, and almost do a murder, on their accused man. Father Brown solves the mystery.'

'I wish these clergymen would solve this mystery.'

'Well, there is a Mr Glass in this story.' And a Father Black, thinks the doctor to himself, but only says, 'That is the Pendennis cottage over there.'

'May I come and see this exorcism, Doctor?'

'Perhaps you will see round it, like Father Brown. He was a visitor from another culture, a Catholic in a middle class Protestant world, solving their crimes with ease. Have you any religion, Glass?'

Glass opened his mouth, and the Pendennis cottage *screamed.*

Chapter 3

'RED-STABBING THE TALL WHITE WALLS THE MAN IN THE ATTIC IN THE RED PLASTIC BAG THE BLACKLACE CARVING THE POPPYCLOUDS OOZE RED FOG OVER THE DEEP SEASEAGULL GLITTERING PARTICLE THE SMALL WINDOWED BOATS SIX WHITE FEATHERS PLUCKED FROM THE PILLOW THE SVELTE CATARACTS OF BUTTER DIPPED IN BLOOD BLOOD BLOOD BLOOD'

And then the roaring ceases suddenly from the face stretched on the rivers of vomit and a little shy voice sings,

'If your house was made of glass
I could watch you whenever I pass
I could look in not out alas'.

'May I have a glass of water, Father? May I have a glass of water, Father John? Some champagne, Father? WOULD YOU LIKE A DRINK OUT OF MY — BOOT, FATHER? What would you like to drink? Blood of Jesus? It runs out of the laceholes. You'd get it down your black frock and on your god-collar. A red round, a dog-collar on heat . . .'

She barks and whines like a hound. She throws off the covers and puppy-noises come from under her skirt.

'Look, John, I've whelped! I'M A BIG GIRL NOW, FATHER. I WANT A PRIEST-CHILD. HAVE A DRINK OF BITCH-TIT. If I had a priest-child I expect it would turn into a PIG.'

And now there is grunting and snuffling and squealing.

'Why a pig, Johnnie? As a priest, you tell me why a pig. Why, because pigs are sacred. Don't you know? Didn't they teach you why pigs are sacred when you were spilling yourself out every night at the seminary? I bet pigs didn't come into your theology books. I'LL tell you why we're sacred. IT'S BECAUSE WE EAT SHIT.'

A great multiple squealing like a sackful of suckingpigs.

'AND ITS BECAUSE OUR PIGLETS DRINK OUR GOOD MILK WHICH IS MADE FROM SHIT.'

'In the Name of Jesus Christ, God's only Son, in the Name of God the Almighty Father and of the Holy Spirit, I command you whose name is Legion, I exhort every evil spirit that without harm each one of you departs from this daughter of God, Joan Pendennis, and that you return to the place that God ordained for you in the burning pit, there to languish forever. . .'

'BURNING PIT? BURNING PIT! DO YOU KNOW WHERE THAT BURNING PIT IS WAS AND WILL BE FOR EVER? LOOK AT ME, PRIESTS.'

Unwillingly the gaze of the two priests, the Rev. John and his much younger companion, is drawn to the bed, on which the girl, Joan Pendennis, has thrown off the covers and on which she is lying, bound down by webbing straps that allow her a limited freedom. Her arms and her legs are spread wide and, as they watch, her grinning face with the bolting green eyes seems to swell.

They know it is swelling, because the eyes get smaller and smaller in an increasing expanse of skin until the countenance fills the whole room. The eyes are like minute flies walking far below on a rink of skin, and then the flies wave at them and they see far below two girls. They are falling straight down and land as on white leather cushions, to find that the girls have taken their hands and are leading them towards the edge of the white rink, which is beating slightly underfoot. Suddenly the floor goes hot and red and transparent, and they look down and see a matwork of red worms squirming deep down through the ground, tangled as far down as they can see and on every side. A terrible heat beats upward. The two eye-girls have led the priests to the rim of the arena and with gestures motion them to stay there. Then they run lightly back, waving as they go, their footprints dimpling the leathery ground. When they reach the eye-sockets, they curl up in them again. The priests look around. Suddenly the ground splits with a bass rumble, gathers itself up, and a ridged purple brink of substance rushes towards them. They stand on its peak, and they look down between immense white stones into a wet red pit whose side is studded with red mushroom-shapes and which lashes about. As the shapes rub together, they make a squeaking sound like a multitude of small animals. The sheer gulf twists away out of sight, and then they hear a rumbling, and a great jet of greeny-black liquid appears, shoots high into the air, and falls spattering all around them. John gasps as some of this liquid strikes the back of his hand; it bums. The lip on which they stand trembles violently and they fall forwards into a stench they could never have imagined.

The tearing and burning that happened after that, they say, is mercifully lost to them, though John has filled a large foolscap notebook with his attempts to describe what he remembers of his adventures through this country, which was the body of the girl. One thing he understood, and discussed with his companion, Tom, who retained very much less of the experience, was that the burning and tearing was love. There was so much he saw that he did not yet understand. At one point he saw winged beings flying through netted walls of labyrinth towards a red light, and he heard them singing not out of fear, as one would expect of the damned packed in legions in the body of a possessed girl, but in gladness. Later he lighted on a book which explained to him that these were the molecules of substance joining the comity of a new body, and John thought that they would be released from the memories of their last existence and joined into a new one, like souls released from purgatory. The book opened this world to him; it was an imaginative reconstruction by a scientist of what it would be like to attend the service in the cathedral that was the nucleus of a cell dividing in the red petals of a rose, in a state that would allow one to both hear and see all the vibratory wavelength of the immensely complex molecules.

'The whole nave is bathed in the dim light of a thousand different rainbow shades . . . We are about to witness the mass of replication . . . a sequence of a special kind that constitutes the macromolecule that we call a protein . . . we hear over and over again the special bell-like tones of the phosphorus atoms . . . These chords are echoing not only in the cell of every rose, in the cell of every flower, in the cells of every kind of plant and tree, but in the cells of bacteria, of animals, and of every human being . . . The tempo of the symphony accelerates and there are trumpet calls from behind the veil of the altar. . . .'

On this journey the Rev. John was pierced through and

through with torments that he experienced then as the pains of hell, but which he now believes were the vibrations of life, and he himself was so far away from his natural instincts that he was unable to hear them for what they were. Then again, had it not been for later events, he would have believed that it was the ultimate temptation to wish to be one and many with these rainbow molecules that sang so sweetly within the cataclysm of sensation.

He remembered a landscape of red mountains and lava that was slipping away beneath his burning feet, of trying to run and being overwhelmed by lava, of being ejected from the earth, and of sitting on red rocks that glittered as they cooled and became masses of rubies. Then he came to himself and found that he was chanting automatically, from his book, and staring as he did so at the bleeding vagina of the young girl straddled on the bed in front of him.

'In the Name of Jesus Christ Our Lord In the Name of Jesus Christ Our Lord In the Name of Jesus Christ Our Lord.'

'Give me some water, Father. Please give me a glass of water to drink, Father . . .'

From beside him came his companion's voice. He turned and saw Tom, priest of the neighbouring parish, his friend, staring at him with black eyes in a chalk-white face.

'Beware, John. Whatever you and I just saw, remember the last time, and the bloodshed . . .'

'Tom, I see blood being shed in front of me now.'

That is *disgusting.* This is a demon we are exorcising, or so you told me. He is the master of lies and illusions.'

'GIVE ME SOME BLOOOOOOOOOD TO DRINK FATHER.' The voice modulates down to bass on the word 'blood'.

'I NEED BLOOD TO DRINK BECAUSE THIS THING BETWEEN MY LEGS IS SUCKING THE BLOOD OF MY HEART. I FEED IT LIKE MY CHILD BUT I AM SO THIRSTY FOR LOOOOOVE.'

'Christ be with you; Christ within you;
Christ before you; Christ behind you;
Christ without; and Christ within.'

'MAN BE WITHIN ME. I'M A BIG GIRL NOW BUT I'M FULL

OF BROKENNESS. I'm full of broken glass, and in every sliver there is an image that howls and roars. Heal me Father. Can't you heal me? Come into me I WILL CUT YOU ON THE BROKEN MIRRORS. Broken glass, its number is legion, broken thoughts, broken love, broken reflections. I'm the Ark of the Covenant, Father Noah. Do you know, Father, I'm full of animals that cry out against the great storm and the sea that is like a corpse-cake that keeps on slicing itself into waves full of bodies and drowned animals, I don't want to drown so love me by touching me, bring me together Father by touching my skin, stroke me together Father the sea is so bitter and the water salt as blood that is so salt and thirsty. It is not hell-fire I dread Father it is blood. I am drowning, Father, my animals are drowning . . .'

'Oh God, the preserver and defender of men . . .'

'Men! yes! I'd rather have any animal than a man like you. Something to weld me together, I am a leaking boat, and I am blood-leaking.

Dog be with me; swine within me
Buck behind me; stallion suck me;
Drake snap at me; drone cover me;
Bull above me; hog behind me'.

'John! she is reaching the height of her power. The room is rocking like a boat! Do you not feel it? Keep to your book, John! With me.

'Oh God, the preserver and creator, look upon thy servants and save them. Oh Lord, drive back from us the powers of the demons . . .'

'GIVE ME A GLASS OF HOLY BLOOD TO GLUE ME TOGETHER FATHER I AM DISSOLVING IN THIS OCEAN WHICH IS ROCKING US ALL DOWN TO HELL ROUND AND ROUND AND DOWN AND DOWN LIKE DREGS WASHED OUT OF GOD'S CUP . . .'

For John the room was indeed as the demon spoke whirling round and round as though she commanded the storm, and he felt that he was sinking for the last time. He looked down, and as he looked it seemed to him that the carpet-pile grew taller, like savannah grass, and that if he kept on looking down it would grow taller to receive him, and he would dwindle as he fell so that he would be everlastingly falling past the stalks of red grass. So he looked up, and kept looking ahead, and, once again, it was only later events that made him sure of what he had seen, and the meaning of what he had seen.

It seemed to him that a black man who was a giant burst into the room, and this giant had been runnning a distance as his body was gleaming with sweat and his eyes were bolting white in his head. The nostrils were flared and he was bare-footed and naked save for a red loin-cloth. As he came through the door it was like someone bursting a barrier with his chest, like a tape at the end of a race. He swerved abruptly, and began to run against the direction of the room's whirling. As he ran, he did not change his position, but the speed of the room's turning began to slow until, with a lurch, its contents settled into their ordinary positions. Then the black man stood in the bellowing sound from the demon's bed and opened his great mouth and uttered what John can only describe as 'black sound'. It had the effect of blanketing the demon's wailing, as though he had sent out waves of cancellation across his rival's calling. As he spoke, gathered up into an effort which bunched the muscles of his shining body, it was as though what he had said piled up behind the silence it was making of the demon's voice. Their voices were locked in hand-to-hand combat. Then John could hear Glass's voice from far away saying faintly at first but growing in strength: 'Be still! Be still! Be still! BE STILL.' There was silence. An animal whimpered. Glass responded with a growl like a panther, rumbling and low. 'Be still.'

Then John saw that two ordinarily dressed people, one of them a black gentleman, had come into the room and were standing by the bed. He knew the doctor well; but the other man he had never seen before, and as he laid eyes upon him he hated him at once. 'This is Mr Glass,' said Dr Pocket.

'Look where those straps are cutting the girl, John. It is time to put an end to these barbaric medievalisms!' The doctor stepped forward and felt the girl's pulse. She was quite passive to his hand on her wrist, moving her head slightly. His professional eye ran over the sordid bedclothes with evident contempt and distress.

'If you'd seen what I've seen, Dr Pocket, you would not touch that girl so carelessly. I'd rather put my hand in a lioness's mouth!'

'What have you seen, John? You look all in, both of you. Are you sure of what you have seen? Have you been seeing what you expected to see?' He drew the bedclothes over the Pendennis girl.

'I've seen what I will tell you in due course. I think it is beginning to happen again. You shall see it too . . .'

The room had started to turn and the girl on the bed had raised her head and was glaring at the black man. As she spoke, the room's walls sped past in a blur.

'GLASS! Hah! That's a joke. MISTUH GLASS, HE COME IN, SHINING UP DE ROOM WID HIS GLITTERING EYE. Let me see whether I can shatter your composure, Glass. Are you sharp, Glass, will you draw blood? Shall I drink you dry, have you red blood in you, or Jesus-wine, Glass?'

Suddenly, the Pendennis girl spoke in dead Alex Bodkin's voice: 'Help me for God's sake, Glass. I shall keep my head if you help me. It is swimming on a river of blood.' Now the demon spoke, turning her head towards the Rev. John, and winking at him broadly, though he did not understand why until much later.

'Reflect, Glass. When did you get out of prison? I see you sitting at your prison table, with your head held like glass in your hands. I know you sang silently in your cell, Geoffrey. I —all of me — we are prisoners in the cells of this child. Do you know the song we should sing, together, Glass? I know what song you sang. We all know this song. It is the only song we do know. Can you teach us a better? Hear all our cells sing it, like a hive of glass humming all together. It goes like this, doesn't it, Geoffrey?'

Now the demon sang on her own, then with herself, then in a quartet, then in an octet, and then the parts duplicated themselves, multiplying geometrically until the sound of it beat against their ears in a rhythm that was like the beat of every glittering drop in the sea, then like the beat of a battering ram.

'MISTUH GLASS SAT-AT-A-TABLE MISTUH GLASS SAT-AT-A-TABLE MISTUH GLASS MISTUH GLASS SATATATABLE MISTUH GLASS SATATATABLE MISTUH

GLASS SATATATABLE MISTUH GLASS SATATATABLE SATATATABLE'

John threw his hands against his ears to shut out this beat, but it thumped up through his feet into his body and he began to call out to drown the sound but he could not bear to hear himself. Then, once again, he sensed rather than heard black sounds thrown against the billows of the demon's chant, cancelling them: 'Be still! Be Still! BE STILL!' and he thought how Jesus had first rebuked the wind and the sea, and then sent the demons into the herd of pigs, that ran over the cliffs into the sea.

But Jesus was not a black man with white eyes and a red loin-cloth running after a woman who taunted and jeered at him crying out 'Catch me, Glass! Mirror me if you can,' darting into a thicket from which a white hound leapt, the black man running after and changing as he did so, falling on four legs and catching the bitch-dog, and coupling with her with many yelps and cries that were also words and phrases and pictures. John saw all the animals chasing and coupling in his vision, the black man and the lady mating among them in many fashions which he knew were called after the names of the animals, and he saw them copulating as porpoises in the sea, and as fishes, and as whales with their mighty bodies leaping clean out of the ocean, and as horses and as birds and as all manner of insects, the black and waxy-polished flying ants in their swarms, and the doomed flight of the dusky drone with his shining queen. It was the sounds of the bees that now predominated, as though the insistent and pounding rhythm of SATATATABLE SATATATABLE had speeded up to a single vibratory Om, the golden sound of the hive, containing all other sounds. And beyond them all he saw the black man and the white woman, through the swimming, flying, running swarms of all-living that cleared, and he saw the black man disengaging himself from the little girl on the bed where she had been bent with her back to him as they coupled. And then he saw nothing of the kind, but listened as he thought the two spoke, though he could not see that they spoke as he heard them, mature woman and her lover, he only saw a black man whom he hated bending over a little girl on a bed whose webbing restraints he was gently untying.

'Geoffrey. Geoffrey Glass. A black man! How black you are, Geoffrey. Are you still afraid of me?'

'Afraid of you! Afraid of the world I live in? We have been out hunting together.'

'White Lady, Black Gentleman. Kiss me.'

And John saw the black man bend to kiss the little girl on the bed. As he did so, the doctor and the priests called out.

'Mr Glass! She is dangerous!'

'A maniac, Mr Glass. The strength of ten.'

'The danger is not over yet.'

And he heard himself saying, 'If you had seen what I saw.'

And he heard the black man he hated say:

'Let me undo these cruel straps at your feet. Can you get up?'

And the little girl reply:

'I shall walk in your ways. Blessèd be your feet that brought you here.'

Interlude

O she looked out of the window,
As white as any milk,
But he looked into the window,
As black as any silk,

Hulloa, hulloa, hulloa, hulloa, you coal black smith!
O what is your silly song?
You never shall change my maiden name
That I have kept so long;
I'd rather die a maid, yes, but then she said,
And be buried all in my grave,
Than I'd have such a nasty, husky, dusky, musty, fusky,
Coal black smith
A maiden I will die.

Then she became a duck, a duck,
A duck all on the stream,
And he became a rose-combed drake,
And he loved her back again.

Then she became a hare,
To run upon yon hill,
And he became a long-legged buck,
That boldy did her fill.

Then she became a turtle dove,
To fly up in the air,
And he became the second dove,
And they flew on pair by pair.

Then she became a mare, a mare,
That canters on the meadow,
And he became the stallion
To ride upon his fellow.

Then she became a two-lipped flower
          This never was wrong,
While he became a honey-bee
          And filled her with his song.

Hulloa, hulloa, hulloa, hulloa, you coal black smith!
          O what is your silly song,
You shall never change my maiden name
          That I have kept so long;
I'd rather die a maid, yes, but then she said,
And be buried all in my grave,
Than I'd have such a nasty, husky, dusky, musty, fusky,
          Coal black smith
                    A maiden I will die.

Chapter 4

'That's a trick worth knowing,' said Dr Pocket. 'Where did you learn it? A form of hypnotism?' All that the good doctor had seen was his friend bending over the Pendennis girl's bed, speaking some words which apparently pleased her, and touching her face rhythmically. 'A form of hypnotism, I dare say. The words you use are part of a traditional ballad, aren't they? I've heard them sung on the radio.' The doctor walked on a few paces, then stopped. 'You know, my drugs and injections were no good, and the priests' meddling was downright dangerous; but your little song just hit the spot. They tell us doctors not to dabble in psychiatry, you know; and the exorcism service expressly forbids the priests from 'conversing with the demon' as they call it. Yet all real cures come from 'conversing with a demon'. Drugs are supposed to be safe, and they're not: often the side-effects of them are worse than the original illness they're prescribed for. Religious services are supposed to be not only wholesome but safe also, yet the Church doesn't really seem to have a grasp of the subject of demons. Doing what you did with that girl is said to be the most dangerous thing you can do when dealing with a demon, yet it worked.'

'Perhaps it is the most dangerous thing for a Christian priest,' said Glass.

'Very bold, at any rate, Geoffrey. You said you had studied. With Jung perhaps, or Layard, or Estabrooks for hypnotism and suggestion, or perhaps . . .' Here he paused.

'You were going to say "perhaps with some African witch-doctor". I can see through you, Dr Pocket.'

'I can't see through you, Glass. Not yet, anyway.'

'I did have a teacher.'

'Forgive my asking, was he black?'

'You are right to be interested in the colour of people's skin. No, in fact he was white. And red. And the red blackened. Then I had another teacher, though he was more like a judge and an examiner. He showed me how to study alone, sitting at my table.'

'The table! Like the one at the cottage. Like a river, not frozen, but living, and moving very very slowly as the eyes move along the grain and see the pattern. I remembered that as you were telling me about the meaning of your name.'

'It is good for a man to possess something that reminds him of the meaning of his name.'

'But can you tell me what the little girl was saying about prison? Was that a fantasy or a metaphor about her psychotic state?'

'She was taunting me about what I was. I will tell you the whole story one day.' Now Glass stopped on the path, raising his head and smelling the air with his great nostrils. His eyes flashed back at the doctor. 'There's something still in the air, Dr Pocket. Something much bigger than what has already happened. I wish you would go home and stay by the phone. You will be needed later on today. The moon is dark and the movement is gathering power.'

'Dark moon? Does that mean anything?'

'Only that the time has come round again.'

⋆ ⋆ ⋆

The village hall at Petroc was a substantial pantiled brick building that had been donated in the 1930s by some member of the Box family, who had once owned the village. It would be the first building of Petroc that you met, if you happened to be toiling up from the valleys, where the twin streams streaked through the grey rocks and black soil. If you were a visitor from the outer world, and coming down the hill off the moors, you would have passed the inn, a row of shops, the church, set back from a little market square, a garage, a builder's merchant, and a short stretch of hedgerow, before you came upon the concrete platform on which the hall was built, with the splendid view from its tall back windows over Petroc valley.

Framed in this view at this moment was a small committee on a slightly raised dais at the end of the big inner room. The members were Mary Cuttance, the Rev. John's wife, blonde, fair-skinned, a bit sensitive to the cold and thus bundled up in a big cream-coloured fisherman's jersey, and Miss Box, a skinny spinster with a regal manner, who lived in one of the tiny church-cottages with her minute poodle, that was even now scratching at the table behind which the committee sat. Their chairman was Muir Mostyn, tall, white-haired, weather-beaten, whose rangy anatomy concealed a very diffident and sensitive nature. He published nature-notes in a London newspaper, and an occasional poem in the literary journals, and had something of a name as the local poet. He was a widower. It was said of Miss Box that she had to be that skinny to get into her bedroom at the narrow little cottage, and that there was no room for her dog in there, and he had to sleep in the washbasin; and that since his wife died Mr Mostyn the poet had not sold any of her clothes, since he liked to wear them himself. They did not know what to say about Mrs Curate, now Mrs Acting-Vicar, except that she was a 'chilly mortal' and probably not very good in bed, which on balance was preferable in a clergyman's wife, and accounted for John's hungry look, and put hell-fire into his Sunday sermons.

Facing them was an audience of about fifteen people of the village, looking rather lost among the rows of wooden seats set out for the concert on Sunday. The paraffin stove in the corner reeked cosily. The hall had been very solidly built by those builders of the thirties, who were brought into the village to do the job. This was still a bone of contention, and a whole set of village people would not enter the hall because of the Box family's refusal to use local craftsmen. The meeting had been in progress for about half an hour, and was getting nowhere.

'Ladies, we shan't get far if we use emotive language like "The Plague of Demons" or "The Curse of Petroc",' said the chairman. 'We are here to find cures, not curses. Mrs Trevelyan.'

Molly Trevelyan was making the most of her mourning, after what was admittedly a very distressing experience, yet still the most exciting thing that had ever happened to her. She wore a black veil, and wiped her eyes under it with a white handkerchief held in black-gloved fingers. Her eyes were particularly heavily made-up, and she had been crying, which left tracks in her powdered cheeks. The mascara was smudged. Behind her veil she looked awesome and dangerous, like a cracked statue.

'What I want to say, Mr Mostyn, is that it's no use being all *poetical* about it' — here she simpered, as she knew that her small audience would take her emphasis to refer to Mostyn's supposed effeminacy. She could not resist repeating this effect. 'We all respect your *poetry-writing*, but this is life and death. My little girl is lying there in the churchyard a stranger to me and she was the third death in the village. Joan Pendennis I've heard is better and all because of a black man who talked to her, but we can't rely on gossip or strangers. My little Rose is dead and if her dying means anything we've got to stop it happening again.' Molly Trevelyan sat down heavily, dabbing at her face through her veil to a light rustle of sympathetic applause.

'You're quite right, Mrs Trevelyan,' said the chairman mildly, And I don't suppose you'd find anybody in this room to disagree with you . . . . Mrs Anchorage?'

Mrs Anchorage was a young grandmother who lived with her husband, a retired merchant-navy captain, in a bungalow on the edge of the moor. It was known that she had brought up and sent out into the world a large family who came back to see her each Christmas; the overflow, which grew greater each year, took rooms in the inn. She said, loudly and firmly, 'Well, I disagree with Mrs Trevelyan for one! How do we know that it isn't some purely medical problem, even you could say an emotional problem. Something new that emerged at these little girls' puberty, as they became women. Girls become women too young nowadays, and don't know what to do with themselves . . . ' she glared at an anonymous *sotto-voce* that remarked that it could tell them, all right. 'All these girls were the same age or thereabouts, and I've heard of little girls going very strange at their first periods if their families or teachers are too shy to give them sex instruction or to tell them what's happening — yes,' she said, raising her voice in anticipation of the murmur that came in response to her use of the words 'sex' and 'period', 'sometimes a girl thinks she's hurt down there when she starts, and it's a time when all children get strange fancies and tell themselves extraordinary stories. It's up to their parents or the proper authorities to give them sex instruction, and it's high time there was some of that in the village. It's not all sly gropes and funny sayings, you know,' staring hard again in the direction of the *sotto-voce*. There was a certain amount of restless scraping of wooden chairs as she finished, and one seat went down with a bang. The poodle on the dais yelped abruptly, and Miss Box's hand went down to rumple its stiff little plume of head-hair.

'Ladies! Please — everybody must have their chance to speak.' The chairman thought privately that much too much fuss was being made. Certainly, for a small meeting, this one made a lot of noise with its chairs and the poodles. 'We shall not solve this problem if we ignore any possibility, however distasteful.' To his relief a strongly masculine voice now spoke up, very burred. Gideon Twig considered it a part of his constabulary duties to maintain the local accent in his mode of speech. He would loom in the dusk of the street upon some pair of lovers and wish them 'good-night' like the voice of the village itself. Most people considered him an old phoney, and preferred to talk more like the telly. Even his cronies, the fishermen of the harbour where the twin valleys united and debouched into the sea, no longer talked in the old way, not until they had had a few pints. Mr Twig was a much more sensible and well-read man than most of his fellow-villagers, who 'educated' themselves with the aid of the telly. He himself would not have it in the house.

'Mr Chairman, I propose that we form a sub-committee to write a report to the local health authority describing the facts and expressing our fears of an epidemic of madness. We must enlist the assistance of the vicar, Mr Bodkin — no, he can't help, he's dead — the Rev. John' — with a stately nod to Mrs John on the platform — 'Dr Pocket, who is not here today, I see, and others, to explore every possibility, including faulty sex instruction at school' (the cries of protest were really very strident, thought Mostyn) 'or at home' (now that really amounted to a shriek of rage, thought the chairman, as he tried to take down what Gideon Twig was saying, and he looked up and down the rows to see who was making that penetrating sound) '. . . natural LSD in the drinking-water, in some school fountain or in some hidden spring or fountain frequented by schoolchildren for a dare, ergotism . . .' (why *did* an unusual word make some people so angry, wondered Mostyn) 'infected wheat that has gone mouldy with a powerful drug, and whatever else . . .'

Mostyn raised his silver propelling-pencil and pointed towards

Gideon. 'Is that a formal proposal, Mr Twig? Will anybody second?'

A new voice interrupted him. 'I think we should discuss the matter further before forming some male-orientated committee to meet in secret, Mostyn. You have not between you exhausted the list of possibilities,' said Sylvia Pendennis, standing up, in her black fur-coat ('dyed mouse' as the lady behind the counter at the grocer's had once put it).

Sylvia Pendennis, the mother of Joan Pendennis, whom Geoffrey Glass had rescued so strangely (according to the Rev. John), and so efficiently and gently (according to Dr Pocket), was a woman who had acquired an air of mystery in the village. Born and bred there, and attending the village school, in the times when there was one (now the children were collected in a bus to go to the big new school on the moors), she had been a star pupil. This meant that she had eventually to go to the grammar school at Bodwell. Scandal of scandals, the whole family moved there, keeping on the house in Petroc and renting to summer visitors. Then, remotely, she had gone to Cambridge, taken a brilliant degree in Law, read for the bar, and then she became famous, not only in Petroc but at large, since she took silk, one of the few women at that time to become counsel. She prosecuted a number of not very interesting cases as a junior, and then somehow drifted out of the public's attention, surprisingly, since she had had a particular association with murder trials. It was supposed that instead of setting up in the more lucrative role of defence counsel, with the glamour of a Portia, she had preferred to prosecute murderers and murderesses as subsidiary counsel to more famous leaders, and thus lost the limelight. Her course seemed sordid, yet unexciting, so the reporters forgot her. Then it was heard that she had left the courts, and had a child. It was this child that she had brought back to Petroc. She cleaned up and altered the family home, modernised it, and settled there with her Joan and a library of books. They were not law books, however. They were books on psychology and the occult.

'What do you mean, Mrs Pendennis?' said Mostyn wearily, not venturing to point his silver pencil at the lady lawyer.

'You of all people — a poet! — should know something about

the history of this place. It is not the first time this has happened here!'

'What has happened here — exactly, Mrs Pendennis?'

'A Plague of Witches, Mr Mostyn.'

At this there is a murmur of surprise from the audience, but a murmur that seems to linger a little longer than one would expect, to go on a little insistently, a little breathily, with something of a rumble to it (that must be Mr Twig) and something of a wail underneath it. The vocal landscape is complicated at this moment by the fact of Sam Treadle taking his sheep and his sheepdog Mossy out along the road and into the next field, as he always does at this time of day, the late afternoon. Miss Box's poodle stands up stiffly and yaps twice at the sound of the sheepdog. The sheep bleat outside, in the distance, and the sound finds a sketchy echo in the restlessness of the audience in the village hall. The people on the dais look down sharply on their meeting; the sun has begun to enter the window behind them as it sets, and throws its confusing shadows into the hail. The people there are perhaps made uncomfortable by the slight dazzle; their hands are busy and restless about their eyes and faces.

Sylvia is untroubled by the sunlight, since she has left her row and is speaking from an aisle. She knows how important it is to talk to a face and not to a silhouette: learned judge is also a man, if you can see him clearly, even though he is dressed in a wig and a red frock. By shading her eyes she has a convenient excuse for gesturing, even using the slight amplification of a hand cupped at the mouth like a small megaphone.

'Yes, Mr Chairman, a Plague of Witches.' She is a woman who you realise is very small and very slight physically only when you know her well, and the reason for this is that her face is remarkable, and her whole being full of vitality. It is said that when she walked into the Cambridge Union to propose the motion that 'Woman is the Educator, and there is no other' her opponent on the other side of the table, an actor famous for playing arrogant roles, and for his drawl, said quite loudly, '*Who* is that marvellous little fruit-monkey!' She was monkey-like, but very very feminine also. The low brow, the small round head, the slight body, the glossy black hair worn long, the energy of her movements, were all animal, but her gold-green eyes and the intelligence of her face and the expression of her movements were most human. Until this moment Mostyn had wished there were more humans like her. She looked directly at him, and her mouth and nose, which in repose were pushed forward in a kind of delicate muzzle-unit, broke into a smile that dazzled him. He quite forgot that he meant to curtail her speech. He was also glad to be distracted from the slight, almost subsonic, grunts and rustlings that seemed to be accumulating in the room as the shadows gathered and the sun reddened.

'In 1646,' said Sylvia in a dry, clear voice that trod clear over the restlessness and fidgeting of the others, 'Matthew Hopkins, Witch-finder Extraordinary, was summoned to Petroc village by the Ecclesiastical Authorities to put down by the most stringent means a Plague of Witches in the neighbourhood, not only little girls but also mature women and mothers . . .'

The restlessness has turned to responsive attention. There are murmurs of approval and approving grunts, which in the gathering twilight have acquired animal resonance.

'Just a minute. Just a minute, please, Sylvia. Who let that animal in here?'

'What animal, Mr Mostyn?' calls out a mocking female voice.

'A cat, I think. I saw a flash of white among the chairs. Can you see it anywhere? No? Please proceed, Sylvia — Mrs Pendennis.'

'His task was made all the easier for there was a long tradition of witchcraft in the village, and there had been earlier persecutions. Witches were swum in the village pond, and three little girls drowned under the question. Moles and warts were pricked with six-inch steel pins to find out whether they hurt or no. The torture of drinking water forced through a great leather funnel was applied. The extreme pain caused by pressure in the bowels forced a confession. This, the Question Extraordinary, was found most effective.

'Then men formed bands of vigilantes to listen to talkers in their sleep, to listen to old crones muttering in their senility, to spy through hedges on small girls talking confidentially to their dolls — poppets they were called then — and to spy on the restless dreams of young girls shedding their blood of puberty.

'No women were burned on this occasion, but a dozen women died from the tortures, in prison. The oldest was a great-grannie of eighty, the youngest nine years of age. But if they had not died in this way, they would have died in another, for confessions had been taken, and these women would have been burnt for their great energies that men could contain by no other means than banding together and calling themselves "witch-finders".'

Sylvia's voice had risen there, because as she spoke the word 'great energies' there was such a chorus of agreement mingled with the barking of a dog outside, that had she not spoken loudly, her voice would have been drowned. The people in the hall hung on the words she spoke, and moved with them, swaying on their chairs and gesturing with their hands. There was a constant hum of people's low voices among the shifting and rustling of feet and chairs. Alone of all the audience, Gideon Twig, who could just be seen by the bulk of his body and the stolidity of his pose in the front row of chairs, immediately by the dais, was unmoved. As Sylvia speaks now it becomes like a revivalist meeting, when the more felicitous of the minister's remarks are greeted by holy calls and sung phrases from his congregation.

'And the confessions spoke of round dances, the Wild Hunt, and the great dark man of the coven.'

At the raised table now there were three dark shadows outlined on the sun's disc that was sinking behind the wooded ridge of the valley. The middle one bent forward.

'Sylvia,' said Muir Mostyn, 'is this quite germane? These are enlightened times. There is no Matthew Hopkins now.'

'Oh yes there is. But listen to what it is called. It is called — the National Health Service!' The room seems fuller now, the shadows have not shrunk it, but have made its outlines and limits indefinite, and seem to have added to the audience, to have filled the rows of chairs with attentive figures.

'Let me ask all the women here to be completely honest. How many of you have been troubled each month by strange fancies, sudden fierce lustful feelings — perhaps for a man you have just seen, perhaps for the girl around the corner — that you cannot account for — dreams of animals, strange chances, like wishing a person would call you on the phone, and at that moment that identical person does! — nightmares of an animal standing under a tree of shadows, and the four-footed beast steps forward into the moonlight, and it has that man's head, and you look up at the moon, and the moon is that same man's face, wearing a hat of shadow and a cloak of shadow, sprinkled with stars.'

The mention of the dark man receives particular enthusiasm, and now there is an occasional lambent light among the figures in the body of the twilit hall, as though somebody has got hold of an electric torch, and is playing with its swinging beam, only the flashes are bluey-white. In them there are glimpses of glaring faces, mouths with the lips blackened in the cold light, hands, a bearded muzzle, which must be Mr Anger, the nursery gardener, as he is present, but seems like a seated bear. The noise now is almost continuous, save where it lowers as Sylvia goes on.

'You have been so tensed up with these energies for which you have no name — you cannot bear the sight of your ordinary meals, you want other food, strange unnamed food, and you can't tell your lawful wedded husband because just now you can't stand his placid unexciting male munching of those oh-so-ordinary meals you are compelled to lay before him (though your hand slips and the scalding soup pours down his trousers — and what does it rouse there?).'

There is an animal chorus of jogging shouts, and there is the clatter of hooves somewhere at the back of the hall, a flurry of sparks where one strikes an iron supporting-pillar.

'And you can't tell the clergyman because the very fact of him being a man with a man God up in the sky loving him and hating women makes you want to tear and scream — and anyway you're not supposed to talk about sexual feelings to clergymen since their God by popular report never had any — so you make an appointment and take the whole thing to your doctor — also a man — and he nods very sagely and wisely and says . . .'

Here Sylvia employs a natural gift she has, that of mimicry. She is able to slip easily and convincingly into an accurate imitation of a man's baritone voice. The atmosphere and the encouragement of her gathering audience, chirping and bumping in the hall, with the increasing darkness, turns her trick into a feat of mediumship. She *is* the doctor, while she is speaking for him. A row of chairs falls with a clatter, and there is a heaving bristly sound near her as of some large animal body dragging itself across the parquet tiles. She feels something barging a little against her side and reaches out a hand: whatever it is has gone in a flash, but it had a cold scaly body, like a frost-chilled oak. These events do not concern her; she is a pattern in the happenings around her and not a separate person, not the lawyer-lady come to put the village right with her experience and forensic eloquence. Though she has these skills she does not know she uses them: she is completely absorbed in her function now, and she is speaking for things that have forgotten over long ages how to speak, and which are gathering in that village hall. She is possessed as truly as her daughter was, but she is a person who has known more, for she has not allowed her mind to be extinguished by her body's energies but has trained one in the service of the other. She is conscious that something is riding her like a mount, but it is a ride by a lover who has entered her and who moves in her, and gathers her energies up with his own, though she does not know or consider whether this rider is human, or animal, or some other. All she knows is that his movements within her are also words, which she speaks, and it will not be long before the climax comes, and everything changes for her and for him. Now she speaks in Dr Pocket's deep tones.

'Do you get these feelings every month, Mrs Pendennis? Just before the period? I thought so. And during it too? Yes, well, there's no problem. We call this thing "the pre-menstrual syndrome" or "premenstrual tension". PMT for short. It is very common.'

Sylvia resumes her own voice, and replies in Dr Pocket's in a dialogue.

'But what is wrong with me, Doctor?'

'There's nothing wrong at all.'

'But I feel so horrible, so tense and frustrated.'

'It's your natural cycle. It's part of being a woman.'

'Is that an illness?'

'Does being a woman seem like an illness to you?'

'It was you, Doctor, who said you could do nothing. Now you are trying to trap me into saying that I hate being a woman.'

'Dear Mrs Pendennis, I am not trying to trap you into anything.

But if you feel so witchy every month, it's not surprising you came to me for treatment. And we can treat it.'

'I did not come to you for drugs. I came to you for an explanation.'

'I have tried to give you one.'

'You have tried to call me a witch, and to condemn me to medicine.'

'You are getting very excited.'

'That's what I came to see you about in the first place. You have now told me that I have good reason to get excited, since you know nothing about one of the most common complaints of all.'

'I'm afraid that is true. But you'll wear yourself out. Let me take your blood pressure.'

Sylvia switches to her own narrative.

'Naturally the blood pressure is up after all that shouting, and unless you are very much on your guard, you are now told that your condition at your age could get serious unless you take such and such a prescription. You might make the mistake of letting on that you have your most extraordinary dreams at these times: dreams of a Wild Hunt, of round dances, of the great dark man of the moon — dreams that the old witches of Petroc were compelled to confess as crimes!'

There is a howl of rage from the hall, and there seem to be very many women present. The flickering light that plays over them, like a silent summer thunderstorm, shows long hair tossing, and clothes that are in tatters; many of the figures appear to have torn their garments open in the front to free their throats. Mostyn believes he is in a dream; he leans over his pathetic committee table staring into the shadowy hall, and he sees throats that swell with animal calls and dancing figures that are moving round and round in a whirling circle, seeming to move the room with them, and he sees babies and animals fed at these breasts as they turn in and out of the circle in a light that is like a flickering cold bonfire.

'You tell your dreams to this man, you tell this ignorant person the advice that comes from the gods!' Now her mimicry is savage and distorted, her woman's voice is a caricature mincing, her doctor the brash, confident, insincere fake masculinity of a toothpaste ad.

'But, Doctor, those terrible dreams. I wish some big stwong Doctor 'oud tell 'ickle me about 'ose howwible bad dweams.'

'Oh, Mrs Pendennis, or may I call you Syl?'

'You make me feel so safe, Doctor . . .'

'It's all the training we have to do to wear one of these white coats and give advice, you know. Well, Syl, not even the psycho-analysts, those great and wise mitteleuropean conquistadores of the mind, can tell us much about these secret women's feelings at these times, I do assure you.'

'Do you, oh great white Doctor?'

'Indeed I do assure you, Little Ms Muffet. The great big spider comes down and frightens you from your curds and whey, but it goes away again, and it is quite harmless.'

'NO DOCTOR IT IS NEVER HARMLESS AND IT NEVER WAS. IT ISYOUR CREATOR!'

'What was that, Syl?'

'Some naughty man let off a bombie in the next street.'

'Is that all? Now let me give you some of my pretty pills.'

'But, Doctor, look, I always seem to be incredibly lucky at these times! I get letters from old friends, I pick up pound-notes.'

'Now I want to speak to you very seriously about these fancies. You must not believe in them. Such things as we all know are impossible. It is a very serious symptom that you are describing.'

Sylvia resumes her narrative, and there is quiet in the room, though something very large has settled down by Mr Twig in the front row, who sits as still as ever, as though he had died of fright, quietly. The bulk of animal that has joined his silhouette seems to be tugging quietly at his still figure, and its breathing is the only sound, until Mr Twig's figure suddenly settles to one side with a slithering noise, and there is a kind of muffled grunt, and a munching.

'So when the doctor begins to threaten you with his "serious symptoms" which are his magic words and spell for causing you to look squinnying at yourself, so you cannot believe what is really there, in you, you clam up in case you have said far too much. But he is still suspicious, so he doles out those little tranquilliser pills which, if you take them, will close up the abyss in you. Have you not wanted to take these pills, to get peace from these ignorant males who cannot tell what glories open up in women, though we freely offer them? Have you not also wanted at the same time to flush these expensive National Health chemicals straight down the toilet, because you know that this monthly abyss contains your most precious things — your childhood, your womanhood, your manhood, your gift of blood and your magic? But have you not also continued, some of you, to take them for weeks, months or years because you know too that you can speak to no man about such things, to no lover, to no authority? Yet you know that men do not change as we do, with the moon's changes, and no man can reach as deeply as we do into the abyss of his being, which as doctor and priest — yes, and even as poet, once the spokesman of these life-changes — which he denies is there. And when we as women meet in these insights and dreams and powers and magics they call us witches, and they torture and burn us!

'Shall I tell you, Muir Mostyn, what I and all these people see in this room and you can listen and then tell me what you see, and we shall know which of us is mad. I see a company of women dancing in their energies round a fire that looks golden to me which they have made by gathering their life energies into a cone and a spirit who will go out and do their bidding. I see joined with them all the animals of the forest, the ghosts of the wolves and bears, the tribes of all the dogs and the pigs and the bees. I see the wheat which returns death to us as nourishment, as the womb within each one of these women is capable of returning the death of former generations into new human life. I see these women creating a Grail Castle, which is the Castle within the Grail that is within each woman, the birth-cone that is everywhere where women are, that you cannot see; the globe in the crescent within the secret place, which changes colour and position with the moon. I see these women raising an energy that will destroy you because you believe that it is ugly, but it is the love that moves the moon and the stars, and which will destroy the world because it is time, unless that world can see itself reflected as in a mirror in the beings that it created that it calls man, and which in love it set above itself. It is now time to depose that arrogance. Give me your answer. Do you see beauty in this dance that we are making, or do you see ugliness, do you see nothing but darkness and animal breath?'

Mostyn was leaning over the table, peering into the shadows of the hall, poking at the darkness with his unseen silver pencil. He had hardly heard Sylvia's impassioned speech, and he had not comprehended the goings-on in the hall, and he leaned over the table and he spoke in his reasonable chairman's voice.

'What are those animals doing here? How did they get into this hall? There is an important meeting going on. It's not market-day today. Can't you tell the cowherd to move them on? There's a noisy dog still herding the sheep! Constable Twig! What has happened to you? Get up, man, do your duty. There's some dog fight in the corridor. There's some bitch on heat in the corridor. I can hardly hear myself speak — get a fire-bucket and souse the bitch-dog in the corridor. Get paraffin and throw it at the filthy fucking dogs. Catch them on fire and let them howl with the torture as they love, jerking in the flames.'

Sylvia's voice continues, ringing out over the other noises in the room:

'One Joan Pendennis, the namesake of my child, in those former days of persecution (and today, today we have the doctors and the madhouses to manufacture madness) told the court that she had been given her familiar by her grandmother . . . ' and here Sylvia's voice makes another remarkable, medium-like change, into the strong village demotic of a former age, 'given in the lykeness of a whyte spotted Catte, and the said grandmother taughte her to feed the sayde Catte with bread and mylke, and she did so, also she taught her to cal it by the name of Sattan and to kepe it in a basket. Item that eury tyme that he did any thing for her, she sayde that he required a drop of bloude, which she gaue him.' She resumes her usual voice. 'Joan Pendennis, age eleven, taught by her grandmother to give her blood easily and freely, in a context of communication with the animal side of herself, her natural instincts, to find the images of her natural meditation of instinct and puberty within her animal totem and her monthly blood — questioned by the extraordinary torture of water through the funnel, drank nine and a half gallons and died of a ruptured bowel but in no apparent pain, calling aloud her visions of a black man peopling the world with animals and wise women. . .'

The committee-table is still frozen like a shadow-play against the darkened window, where some rags of red remain gleaming in the sky. Mostyn is still stretched across the table, reaching into the darkness. Sylvia's declamation reaches its climax, and her voice changes and expands, becomes gruff and animal-like, or shrieks high into almost-inaudibility, as she pronounces the ancient god-names that are the familiar friends of the witches.

'Under the water-torture women spurting like fountains of blood and water revealed the names of their familiars LIZABET VERD-JOLI SATAT SATATA MAITRE PARSLEY VERDELET'

And the company of witches in the hall responded with their own calls, that grew more rhythmical until Mostyn felt the earth beat as with the dancing of gods, and the building tremble.

'MARTINET SATATAT ABRAHEL GRISSEL TISSY GREEDIGUTSATATA
GREEDIGUTSATATA JEZEBELSAT
BLACKMAN EXCRATESATATATABLE
SATATATABLE SATATATATATATABLE
SATAANDTATATASATATATABLE SATATA
SATATA STATATABLE SATATATABLE MR GREY MR RED MR WHITE MR BLACK SATATATABLE MR GLASS SATATATABLE SATATAB LE SATATATAB LE SATATATAB LE SATATATABLE'

Now, to Mostyn, the light *was* a flickering bonfire; he could see the women with their naked breasts, and their children and familiars clinging to their hair, whirling round, dancing. In its light he looked down and he saw the big white cat with its claws in the mess of meat and rib-bones that lay where the solid bulk of Mr Twig had sat. He saw people with animal masks dancing: there was a dog and a lion and a snake-head, and their eyes rolled and saliva dripped from the jaws of the masks, and as these animal-men reared up to dance, he saw the great pizzles between the animal flanks fully-stretched and shining like leather tubes in the firelight. As the whirling figures passed near him he saw golden eyes gleaming and he felt a fingertip touch his outstretched hand (for he was sprawled over this table, reaching towards them, and he could no longer move). As the circle of people and animals dancing together returned again and again he felt their fingers touch his hair and catch at his clothes. The head of a wild ass passed him grimacing and neighing, dancing on its hind legs with its penis jetting urine straight up in the air, and people danced and laughed, wetting themselves in the fine stinking rain. The wolfhead returned again, and it was gnawing at Gideon Twig's bolt-eyed head, shredded into tattered meat except for the face, which had on it the expression of a man in his last extremity, running hard from danger, though Mostyn knows that he had sat with his animal killer like a lover, stolid on his chair.

'SATATA SATATATABLE MRGLASSSATATATABLE SATATATABLE SATATATABLE SATATATABLE.'

The hands had taken his clothes and were pulling him towards the mouths when suddenly a new thing happened. The big doors at the end of the hall burst open, crashing back against the walls, and in a glare of light which also, he remembered, blared like trumpets, he saw a great sandy desert with the sun rising over it. Far away, he saw a little dot, that grew as he watched, first to the size of a gnat then that of a dog running, then he saw it was a black man in a red loin-cloth running forwards and with a whoosh of burning air he bounded into the room over the threshold and the doors banged shut again.

Mostyn felt the people and things that were dragging him to be eaten turning towards this new apparition. He felt himself slither back over the table and fall on to the boards; the chairs to either side of him were vacant, and there was no sign of either Mrs John or Miss Box; he supposed both had joined the dance. He lay peering between the legs of the table at what was happening in the hall. There was a stench in the air which yet had a lift about it, a yeastiness, like straw and animal dung.

In the deafening noise he saw the black man open his mouth, and white light came out of it. First it was a glare, like a flash-bulb's glare extended into a long moment. The noise diminished, and the witches seemed frozen in the attitudes of their dance, but their mouths were still working in their calling and chant.

Then the black man's mouth opened again, and a lancing red light struck out of it, which gradually shaped itself into audible syllables: 'BE STILL' and quieter and more distinct 'Be Still'. The chanting had diminished in volume to nothing more than a whisper: 'Satatatable satatatable satatatable satatatable' with a hissing whisper in it, 'Missssster Glassss, Misssssster Glasssssss' and the voice of the black man came again, 'Dams, you called me and I came. You will need a leader in the dance. The leader of the dance has come. He who dances is not mistaken. You consume, and have been consumed. You wound, and have been wounded. A glass am I to you who discern me. All dance, dance the round all. Grace pipes the round, pace the dance all.'

Mostyn says that the dance now resumed in a different way. While the former was a circling, this was a weaving. Perhaps it was because he had written poetry that he saw it as a poem, and sometimes heard the black man saying words, and sometimes saw the scenes those words told him. The rhythm *satatatable satatatable* was behind the dance, but now it was not like hooves beating on the earth and shaking the building, it had become faster and more sensitive, it became like a drone or hum that rose in pitch and carried the dancers as though on wings, though they were bat wings and veined insect wings, not feathered like angels or eagles. Unlike angels too, the dancers were naked, quite naked, and their flesh seemed to him so clean and so glowing that they danced by its light, and this radiance made him feel so joyful that he wanted to join the dance, and made as if to crawl forward into it, but the heat that was coming from these bodies stopped him. The hum grew stronger and higher in pitch and of itself seemed to make pictures come into his mind, and he saw, as Sylvia had said in her speech, visions of the world in springtime with all the creatures coupling and expressing the earth's song as it neared its lover the sun, and it was as if he saw the African continent, and the black people of it spreading out and providing for all the races of the world, their black being the colour of their vigour, paling as they receded from Africa, from the centre that life had elected for itself.

* * *

The Rev. John had spent his day resting at the vicarage. His wife was off at some meeting, and he felt a thirst for Bodkin's big mahogany-furnished Victorian official manse, and especially the great black-wood bed with all its counterpanes and mattresses and eiderdowns. He could not explain this thirst for Bodkin's place, but he felt he had to go there rather than to his own home. He slept in the great bed, in his vicar's unchanged sheets. He woke in the early evening, with the sense of something to do. Yes, he must pick up Mary from the meeting. He should have gone to it but he was too tired after the week's events. He dressed in his black coat and his clerical collar (his leanness suited the uniform); and he let himself out of the vicarage, and walked briskly downhill from the church square to the village hall. All was in darkness, but they seemed to be singing hymns inside in the darkness. There was a sort of drone, quite strong, like a powerful speaker heard from a distance, intoning psalms, with the responses of his congregation. His pace quickened. People should not be holding services in the village hall, and in the dark too! Yet the sound reminded him of the beehive in the garden of the Trevelyan family. He opened the door and stepped into the lobby. The big inner doors were closed, and now he could hear a continuous shushing or shuffling as if people were walking up and down in their bare feet, and he heard the humming too, though this was oddly magnified, as though some public address system were being used. He grasped the big black iron loop handle, and swung the door inwards. The room was dark, but it was full of people walking and humming. He felt for the switch that would turn on all the ceiling lights, and depressed it, with a sharp little click.

At first he could not understand what he saw. It seemed as though somebody had half-decorated the room, and left all their workmen's litter about the floor, where red paint had been spilt. There were great swatches of paint up the cream walls, and several bundles of drenched rags that looked as though they belonged in pails. Wooden chairs, some of them badly smashed, were piled high in a far corner, like a Guy Fawkes bonfire ready for firing. In the cleared space in the middle of the room were about fifteen people positioned in a circle, walking slowly round, their hands to their faces as if to protect them from the light. At the centre of this circle, standing taller than any of them, and having the blasted impertinence to be staring full into the face of the Rev. John, was none other than that black man Geoffrey Glass, who lived in the ruined cottage and who had in his opinion molested the little girl at the exorcism. The Rev. John pulled his eyes away from the 'buck nigger' (the phrase that was in his mind). He began to see more clearly, and began to identify the bundles of rubbish as torn pieces of meat, some with their clothes still on them. Standing somewhat aside from the circle of people was another black figure, black because of her fur jacket and her black hair, a small and rather monkey-faced woman in her forties who, as he watched and identified her as Sylvia Pendennis, slowly raised her finger and pointed at the black man. As she pointed, the circle of people stepped aside and parted, as though to let the ray from the accusing finger pass to its target, the black man. As they moved he caught their whispering voices. 'Blessèd be. Blessèd be.' And with their eyes turned to the black man, 'Blessed be thy feet that brought thee here'. The Rev. John in the slow process of recognition saw that though the black man wore ordinary street clothes, the people surrounding him and now moving from the pointing finger were clothed in the remnants of street clothes, bloodstained tatters and rags. With a sob John recognised his wife, Mary, whose great cable-knit jersey was ripped up the front, and he moved towards her. Sylvia's voice ringing out stopped him, as she pointed at the black man. 'It's you! You who were a miserable and cruel murderer. It was your atrocity that forced me from the courts to seek love, away from depravity like yours. What are you doing here in Petroc? Is this massacre your work?'

Chapter 5

The atmosphere in the great council chamber at Lambeth Palace is heavy. The assembled clergymen are all smoking. The Archbishop, who says little, smokes instead. John, now a Canon, has been called to give first-hand evidence to this council and nervously sips at cigarettes. The long windows over the river send slanting beams of light on to the great polished council table. 'I wonder if Glass is listening to us from that table?' thinks John in a sudden nervous fancy. He tries to catch the eye of the Archbishop, but the big old man has wrapped himself up in his tobacco-smoke. Earlier, after lunch, John told the head of the Church what he had found out about Geoffrey Glass, from what Sylvia had told him, and then from his further enquiries in London. The Archbishop said he wanted to hear what his senior clergy had to say about the problem before he dropped any bombshells. John wonders whether he should feel like Judas now. He had seen demonstrations of Glass's power — though really, he thinks, he had only seen demonstrations of sympathy — but he felt no allegiance, only hostility, to this man. 'I felt jealousy straight away, as though I were jealous of the little girl I was exorcising, and wanted to do it all myself,' and 'Could it have been the colour of his skin?' he asks himself, as he puffs away at his tobacco.

The lawyer of the Church should have worn a beard, as he had a bad shaving-rash over his neck and under his chin. He had a very thin moustache, like a Wodehouse gigolo, which went very oddly with his clerical black and his purple stock. 'The question is, your grace, *who* is this man?' he said. He got up and stared out over their heads through the window, where he could see the great brown river flowing beyond the embankment. John followed his gaze: on the south bank of the Thames as they were, the river flowed from left hand to right hand, like strength from the unconscious. He glanced at the wooden table again, and thought how like the river's flow and its water-pattern the grains of wood all were. 'He seems,' said the clerical lawyer, 'to have all the women - that is more than fifty per cent of the electorate - in the palm of his hand.'

'Between his thick lips,' said a sardonic-looking clergyman in gaiters, with a black birthmark the size of a fifty-pence piece on the back of his right hand.

'Do you know, this has happened before . . .' mildly and almost inaudibly remarked a little old clergyman, also in gaiters. He had white hair that stood up as though he had once had a fright or seen a holy vision and had not combed it afterwards.

'The question is, do we support or oppose him? We must decide this today,' said the church lawyer.

'It really has happened before,' said the shock-haired bishop.

The sardonic bishop liked to squash the white-haired one. It was the relationship they had. 'I'm sure such a mass-movement depending on the women emanating from a small West Country village has never happened before.'

'Hitler depended on the women,' said his friend, mildly; 'his oratory had the women between his lips.'

'This isn't like oratory. It's something like a litany,' interrupted John. He had taken to interrupting judiciously since they had made him a Canon. He needed to behave in a political fashion now without losing hold of spiritual values, of course: and how could he do that in a room full of the leaders of his church? He thought he should side as much as possible with the quick-witted sardonic man, and be polite in private to the woolly-haired old mystic, who surely was incapable of bearing any grudge.

'Well, if it's a litany it's not illegal in this country, where we have freedom of worship,' said a very fat clergyman sitting near the door. 'But it's still poaching on our preserves, and with the murders it looks worse than blasphemy.' The woolly-headed bishop looked surprised, as if one could not have anything worse than blasphemy. His sardonic companion watched him with fond contempt, put his finger to his lips, and hushed him. Wool-hair had not intended to speak, but the admonitory gesture made him retire even further into his cushions. 'Petroc, is it called? What happened to the rest of the clergy there? Couldn't they contain this sort of thing?' asked the fat bishop.

'Dead, my lord,' said the sardonic one.

'What?'

'Dead.'

'Oh, dead.'

There was a pause. The little old bishop took advantage of it. 'What I mean is given in Matthew 12.24,' he said.

'Oh, God! *Scripture*,' groaned his friend.

'But when the Pharisees heard it, they said, This fellow doth not cast out devils, but by Beelzebub the prince of the devils. And Jesus knew their thoughts . . .'

'Oh *God*,' said his friend, registering with upturned eyes that the old man was now in full flight, and therefore unstoppable.

'. . . And said unto them . . . if Satan cast out Satan, he is divided against himself . . . But if I cast out devils by the Spirit of God, then the kingdom of God is come unto you . . .'

There was a much longer pause, which the lawyer broke with an exasperated 'But we *can't* announce a Second Coming! Besides — he's black!'

The sardonic one had lost his temper and his poise: 'Yes! Black! And those so-called disciples of his. All *women!* Going about casting out devils like *scripture* of all things! Emptying asylums. Healing madness. Putting highly-trained psychiatrists out of business. Sending the doctors to ignorant village women for training! Holding *conversations* with *animals* at the London *Zoo* on *television*. Going about saying "Blessèd be" and calling themselves "witches". Yes, we ought to burn the whole pack of them, and would probably, but they seem to have power over the courts, what with their confusions and accidents, testifying that their people sometimes die by "self-mutilation" and it's no fault of theirs that this happens. They were all acquitted stock-free from the murder enquiries after that massacre down there at Petroc. Are they above the law? If they are, what can we or anybody else do? What about the woman MP who insisted on taking her snake draped round her like a garment into the House of Commons, and claimed it was her "boa" when the Speaker objected to pets. I saw her put the Chancellor off by letting that *creature* open her dress and suckle her during question-time. Her party put her up to it! It seemed like a dead skin when she wore it, and yet it suckled her, I swear! "Blessed be!" Why not "how do you do" like everybody else?'

But this outburst had only stimulated his friend, whose wrinkled cheeks were glowing and eyes sparkling. John thought that the old man was actually the most up-to-date cleric there. 'This is Homeric! You remember that Circe turned Odysseus' companions to swine, but then they rose up after that "goodlier than before". It is like the doctors of the sixties who took LSD with their patients. It enabled them to converse in mad-language with patients who had been catatonic for years, because they were unable to communicate their extraordinary perceptions. Hearing their doctors *speak* as they thought, woke them all up and cured cases that had been tended as helpless for years!'

His friend was not pleased. 'This is *not* like the doctors of the sixties. This is a political force. You didn't get any of those cured madmen getting into parliament. But come the next election we shall have a black Prime Minister and a totally female Cabinet. What will the United States say; what will Russia think!'

The lawyer was drawn into this against his will. 'They might say nothing and think nothing. They might just join Glass and his gaggle.'

There was another pause. The little shock-haired cleric had used up his energy, and when he spoke it was in a whisper.

'The elder brother of Jesus . . .

'Speak up, Cedric,' said the sardonic one with the birthmark, recovering his poise now that his friend had lost his energy.

They used to say that the elder brother of Jesus was a black man.'

The lawyer had no time for recondite learning. 'As I was saying . . . Why should other nations not join? Why should Glass's movement not become worldwide? He has everything going for him. Single-handed, it seems, he has invented a new religion — or uncovered an old one. And it works — everybody can see that it works. The mad become sane. The sane go mad and come out of it saner than they went in. A few people apparently tear themselves to bits in their ceremonies. Then there is the most powerful suppressed majority in the world — the women. They have suddenly been freed from patriarchal religious authority. They have come into the ancient knowledge of themselves. Moreover, they have accepted a representative of the virile and knowledgeable black races as their leader — no, more their companion in these mysteries, though how he acquired his knowledge is beyond me . . .'

'Great is Diana of Ephesus! Acts 19.34.' A new thought had brought energy.

'Great *God,* Cedric,' rejoined his friend, as of habit, having now recovered his pose of weary negligence, sitting with his leg swinging over the arm of his deep chair.

'No, Great *Goddess!* Diana's statue in the temple of Ephesus revolved, it is said, and had four faces. The face that showed during the dark of the moon was a man's face, and it was black. At this time the goddess also wore a beard, white as wool, and a white owl perched on her shoulder. A human baby suckled at her multiple breasts, in company with a lion-cub, a snake, and a piglet. Though she was sow-breasted at this time, her genitals were those of a man, but wrapped from view in a bloodstained bandage. Then as the moon's light grew into its first quarter, the statue was turned, and the young goddess appeared, slender and lithe, with small breasts and a child's vulva. At the full moon the statue had turned back to front to show Matrone, the fully-pregnant goddess, radiantly white and dome-bellied, except for a tiny black clitoris. Then as the statue turned, her fourth face was shown, that of an old wrinkled woman, with a pair of breasts hanging like wrinkled hose, and on her left shoulder perches a dark man-child's face with no body, but with owl-wings outstretched where ears should be. Her gesture points to this face, and to her slack belly, as if to say that he has flown up from down there, and has perched on her shoulder, where these thick lips whisper counsel into her ear. Then as the month comes to its dark again, she is shown united in one person with her son, as I have told you.'

'Oh, Holy *Shit*! Now we *are* looking backwards.' Sardonicus crackles with disgust. His friend continues.

'And if Satan rise up against himself . . . he cannot stand . . . . But he that shall blaspheme against the Holy Ghost hath never forgiveness . . . Mark 3. 26-29. Gentlemen! I'm worried about the sin against the Holy Ghost.'

Another pause, into which the saturnine bishop dropped his

masterpiece for the afternoon. 'You always were, Cedric,' he said, with an elaborate drawl. They had been at school together.

Nobody laughed. They were listening to Cedric.

'But if we are *wrong* about this man! If he is filled with the Holy Ghost and the Spirit of God, then, if we oppose him, we blaspheme.'

'Be your age, Cedric.' A feeble sally from his schoolfricnd.

'But can we on the other hand not oppose him without bringing the Church totally into disrepute?' This was the lawyer.

The fat man by the door chimed in. It seemed to him to be his turn for learning and poetry. 'There is also the question of his name. That seems like a sign. But a sign pointing which way? Sinister? Dexter? Left? Right? Good? Evil?'

'Or straight up.' Cedric's friend was not being listened to.

The fat cleric resumed. 'Glass, Geoffrey Glass. Let me see. Something brittle. Shatterable. Impenetrable. Unyielding. Revealing. Concealing. Reflecting. Distorting. A glass bell-jar for madness. A crystal palace for a mad king. A black mirror for scrying. A glass full of wine? Beetle-black wine, black as cockchafers? A Grail of Glass, full of blood of the Resurrection? A Glass of ancestral spirits? What is it that is in his celebration of the menstrual period, the Devil's Graal of the Witches, that he has stolen from our church lore? Is it that we give power to the men, and he restores power to the women? We, the Church, can handle the women. We have done so for two thousand years. If we can persuade the women that they do not need him, then we have robbed them of some image of a lost side of themselves, and we can shut it away again from them. No woman is fit to govern, gentlemen. But do you see the way the rhetoric is taking us? This man knows something about blood and about the monthly period, the so-called time of the moon, and something about animals and dancing and suchlike, and he in himself has been made by these things, or by his own power, into an image of what they missed in our good Lord, as we have remade Jesus for the benefit of our own rule of law — wait!' (the lawyer seemed to be ready to protest) 'I am simply putting a case. Do you not see the rhetoric? All government is rhetoric and images, and I greatly fear he is in himself the stronger image. We may have to propagandise against this man. Or we may have to propagandise for him . . .'

'Cutting out all the unruly element, of course.'

'Of course, but gradually. Gradually whitening him, so to speak. So he must, this Mr Glass, turn out in the hurly-burly to be either so completely evil that no one could seriously want to be seen with him, or so good that he is a part of the story that we already have, in our own church. After all, brethren, as you see, we already wear much black in our garb, and a touch of white also.'

'And purple.'

'Which is for sacrifice. We can cause him to be all black, and he is powerless; or all white, and he is powerless, and a part of our church too.'

'How can you make him good?'

'We can make him a liberal prophet! Listen: "I am a mirror and who looks at me, whatever good or bad he speaks, he speaks of himself. . ." That is Omar Khayyám, I think. "The perfect man employs his mind as a mirror, it grasps nothing, it refuses nothing, it receives but does not keep . . ." Now you can see where the rhetoric can take us. Our only fear is that he is both very evil and very good at once, like life itself, and then we are lost!'

'A mirror I am to thee that perceivest me,' gently. 'Who on earth said that, Cedric?'

'Jesus.'

'It's not in the Bible, Cedric.'

'Apocrypha.'

'Oh. Ah.'

All this time the Archbishop had remained 'folded in a mantle, as one renouncing the vanities of this world' as the Koran has it, but in his case a mantle of tobacco burning in a big pipe, which he now took out of his mouth. He spoke.

'I've heard you all squabbling like children or animals over your various territories, just as I expected, but never mind that. This nursery talk has cleared the air, and perhaps you'll listen to what I have to tell you. There is no problem. We cannot support Glass.'

The fat cleric threw up his hands. He had thought he had a

winner, twisting and turning in his labyrinth. 'But we can use him, sir. He is a force on an irresistible scale. Bigger by far than Billy Graham.'

'No matter. We cannot support Glass. Neither canonically nor from the pulpit. Nor through the media. Nor politically. Nor from our left wing, nor from our right. We cannot support him. He is a vile murderer.'

All the men in the room looked at each other.

There were smiles on their faces, and a *risus sardonicus* on the face of the bishop with the birthmark staining his hand. His friend, the white-headed old mystic, started to weep without a sound. His friend looked at him in total disbelief, shrugged to the room at large, pulled out a large white handkerchief, and pressed it between the old man's trembling fingers.

'Do you not remember the murder of a farmer called Skinner, on the Thames marshes, nearly twenty years ago? Well, I confess I had taken no notice of it myself. It was not the custom then for clergy to keep up with the Sunday tabloids. The murder was so unpleasant and public feeling ran so high that he had to be tried in the provinces. Some of the photographs of evidence were smuggled out and got to the papers; they were very unpleasant indeed. A whole edition of the *Sunday Weasel* had to be scrapped on a court order; there was nearly an acquittal because of mistrial when these photographs got into public hands. Don't you remember, you young men,' turning to John, 'the horrid thrill of the Skinner Murder, as it was called, when you were a child? I remember getting up early to keep my young son from seeing the morning papers when the trial was on! These old murders fade, you know. Yes, he was *that* Glass! He served eighteen years of a life sentence as a model prisoner and was released for good behaviour. Then he retired down to the West Country. It would have been better for him if he had stayed there. All we have to do is to *remind* people at the crucial time. Just *remind* them. The public will do the rest.'

'Poor Geoffrey Glass,' said Cedric, sniffling a little. John thought to himself, it was bound to come out somehow, as he watched the great river rolling from left to right across the long, smoky windows. 'Poor Farmer Skinner,' said the Archbishop, sternly.

Then the council in their purple bibs shuffled to the long table and seated themselves to record their resolution, bending their faces to the polished glare, the Archbishop bringing them to order by rapping his knuckles against the solid flow of the wood.

Chapter 6

Like nearly everybody in the civilised world, I saw the television programme, and suffered its consequences. As a writer, I had been interested in the Glass Phenomenon, and I went to one of the local groups a couple of times. I found it impressive, but not overwhelming. I was told that if I wanted to be overwhelmed, I should join the group when the visitors went to one of the loony-bins. Many asylums, by the way, were now standing vacant, having been emptied of their patients at one stroke.

In this group, a rather pretty young woman called Sandy gave her version of some of the events I have already described to you. She told us that Geoffrey Glass, who was not a leader but a 'container', had not discovered the spontaneous meditation at all, but rather 'uncovered' it. Glass himself, though the most advanced practitioner of the method then known, did not like to be thought of as a model of any kind, since he, too, had left the ancestral ways at first. The method was, so Sandy said, known to all African witch-cults at one time, and indeed was still practised in remote parts of Africa, where the white man had not yet proceeded far with his compulsive Americanisations (which were so successful because they were closed systems, and therefore insensitive). Anybody who opened himself to the bee-hum must take care to do it in the right company, she warned, because in that state one could take a wrong impress, like an exposed photographic film. There were going to be expeditions to seek out these ancient cults, apparently.

Sandy said that there were as yet no systematic descriptions of their 'holy' state, but there had always been certain poems containing images that were powerful direction-finders to it when the social and personal conditions were right, being the inspired recollections of certain practitioners that could, so to speak, 'move one along to one's next stage of being'. The Glass Phenomenon was introduced by sound in one's deepest guts, in one's every blood-corpuscle — that was like the humming of a hive of bees. The experience was known to the ancients — was the origin of the meditation-sound *Om* — which could also trigger the spontaneous experience in a person if deliberately resonated over many years, and was reputed to be the chord with which Orpheus enchanted the beasts, in the Hellenic mystery cults. It was the first chord he struck on his lyre, and it meant 'now is the beginning'.

Sandy now went into a kind of explanation by means of science. 'If you understand,' she said, 'how this can be possible, even in the terms of our deteriorated and detached scientific world, even in the images of science, then you will not prevent yourself from entering the experience, by conceptualising against it.' The best subjects were the mad, who were gifted men and women who had been forced into an impasse or into repetitious delusionary episodes (which were themselves always images of the truth) by the contradictions inherent in their situation as especially perceptive people, in a world that feared its evolutionary possibilities. The next best subjects — and this accounted for the popularity of the women's side of the movement — were, surprisingly, women shortly before or during their menstrual periods. Apparently here the contradiction was that the period was a time of heightened inner perception for many women, yet, by custom and menstrual taboo, they were not 'allowed' this inner-going or taught the kind of attitude or techniques that would reveal its qualities. The great conspirators against women here, it appeared, were the masculine medical scientists, who set up what the young lecturer called 'howlback': a double-bind situation, an escalating feedback on these lines: *I am a woman and I feel horrible so I go to the doctor who tells me I feel horrible because I am a woman and his telling me this makes me feel horrible.* In magic, Sandy said primly, this would be called 'cursing'.

'The way we like to put it,' she went on 'is that we humans are composite creatures, made up of all the stages we have gone through as an evolving species. In the womb, as embryos, we go through all these stages again: sea-creatures, jellyfish, fish, lizard-snake, wild beast, warm-blooded horse-ancestor. And these stages leave imprints and energy-levels in our brains: we have a reptile-brain, the energies of a horse-brain, as well as a man-woman brain. But as a creature we have made such serious social and evolutionary mistakes that these brains that should work together, giving the human all the skills and grace of the animals, have somehow worked loose and become separated from one another. And this is why our history is so streaked with blood and paranoia, our thoughts at variance with our instincts, our wills with our good. What is called madness is when our animal-headed instincts rush back uncontrollably through our bodies, swamping our too-cool upper brains. Wiser cultures,' she now spoke up, since the other members of the group, the experienced ones, had started to vibrate their humming, 'wiser cultures than ours participate in the lives of the animals with their totem-dances and masks, the discipline of yoga is learnt by observation of the animals, the survivals of witchcraft know this wisdom too. In our poem of the Wild Hunt, for instance, our conscious minds shift down into the body and hunt through the countries that are in the body, transforming from one creature to the other . . . it is the secret of the Sphinx, human animal, many creatures in one . . . and puritan people cannot stand the feelings that come, because each person enters these places in himself which are new to him with a sexual pang, and each is a paradise of the senses. Then after the hunting up and down through the levels, which is like the becoming of each of these animals in turn, and coupling in innocent bliss with one's creaturely mate, there is the sound of the bees, which is the sound of making, the vibration of all the cells of the body in one harmony, the bees of life-energy busy in their red honey-comb. It is also the sound the stars make, choiring together. . .'

And suddenly the bee-hum the group-members were making stopped. Into the silence that was left there came to me the absolutely-real picture of a grey animal running through the snow. It seemed to run towards me and through me, and I felt its hot breath on my face, and smelled blood in that breath, rank and deep, mingled with the sweetness of some herb. It had gone in the next instant, but I could see it still, better than I could see that room. Every hair of the animal was distinct, and every six-armed snow-flake that its running flurried; whereas I had to wear my reading-glasses to see the face of the pretty young woman lecturer.

Now the group spoke, or rather chanted, their famous song:

O she looked out of the window
As white as any milk,
But he looked into the window
As black as any silk . . .

The lecturer had explained that we were not to look for any gross effects, such as a possession of the kind that launched the movement from Petroc — though this could always happen — but rather to watch ourselves as the poem was recited.

Then she became a duck, a duck,
A duck all on the stream,
And he became a rose-combed drake,
And fucked her back again . . .

So I gazed into myself.

Immediately, as the black man looked in, in the poem, he did so, into me. I had a very sharp and sudden impression of a coal-black African thrusting his head into my mind. It felt as though he had grasped somehow a sash-window in my chest and thrust it violently upwards, and stuck his head right into my body, and called aloud. The impression, again, was so vivid that I gasped — and clutched the chair in front of me to reassure myself of what was real. The chair felt real, all right, but less actual than what I had just seen, because less important to me, and actually not as vivid either. The black man was so real that it was as though he was illuminated strongly with bright lights, with photo-floods perhaps. I could see little drops of sweat shining in his cap of tightly-coiled ringlets. He had called out as he entered me, and the echo of his shout rang through my body and tingled in my finger-ends, and the maiden's

You never shall change my maiden name
That I have kept so long

seemed an echo of my own inner decision that I would *not* let go, because I knew that I could have gone with the song and become what it was saying, as that note rang in me.

I spoke to the young lecturer afterwards. I told her what had happened, and she turned to me a look of such pleasure that I caught myself thinking that I wished she would be my companion in the song, and all that went with it. She told me that it was a pity that I had not answered this call, because I would undoubtedly have become possessed — by which she meant, she said hastily, possessed by myself, my true self, and have heard and experienced the bee-hum.

'But why a black man? Why is my true self a black man?' She said that that was difficult to explain, and it had nothing to do with the actual presence on this earth of the man called Geoffrey Glass. He was, if you liked, a catalyst. It was partly because human consciousness had started in the black lands of Africa, and we had diverged from those great beginnings. To recover them, white people had to become black. 'And black people?' Black people had their own songs, and understood this one very well — when it was spoken properly, that is. Another reason was that this integration had to do with the increase of body-consciousness. A white man lived very much in his head. To be whole he had to live in his whole body — in particular, to live with the great organ with which that body met the outside world most directly: the skin. It was, she said, of the same origin in the embryo as the brain itself, and, like the brain, was electrical, with rainbowing electro-magnetic currents that played over it all the time and of which we were usually unconscious. So it appeared in our minds, this skin, as a capacious vessel, a blackness. 'What then is its true colour?' I asked, 'The skin's experience of itself is a joyful and living red,' she replied. A person who truly remembers his womb experience of his making, which was of this colour, would be a hero; and a child born with this knowledge would be a kind of Saviour, said Sandy.

It was shortly after this that the television broadcast went out, and the world has not been the same since. Now that the world has changed, for the better, as everyone agrees, our recollections of the strange habits and customs and the terrible compulsive energies of those former times is strongly tinged with satire and affection, as of some eccentric blood-relative who has died as he lived, astonishing us with his helpless enormities. Nevertheless I will try to tell it as it happened, more or less.

The occasion was twofold, which is why nearly everybody was open to its effects. For the more serious, the constantly-impending troubles of the world, in particular the spread of nuclear weaponry, were to be discussed in a new spirit, that of organised religion. There was an important international politico-religious conference on this theme, and its discussions were to be televised. Some of us realised that the politicians drawing on the established Church in this manner merely meant that they had found a new scapegoat for mankind's troubles: anyone, in fact, who lived outside the great established world religions. But the occasion was so notable because at precisely the same time the *other* television channel was to transmit the debut of one of the most important of these scapegoats, the black magic and rock group called Grizzly Glow. There was a polarisation on the air that night, as two opposing forces mingled in the etheric vibrations that surrounded us all, rebounding to every continent on earth from the floating satellites, carrying to our sets the coloured pictures. How our bodies responded to and interpreted these same broadcast vibrations, all of us now know. The viewing public would see the excessively spiritual and the triumphantly nasty, tussling on the air for our souls.

I expect a lot of people behaved as I did: punching the channel buttons and switching to and fro between the two broadcasts. I expect most of us started with the colourful rock show.

Click!

'Hi! Here we are, ladies and gentlemen, for the biggest rock event of this or perhaps any other year in the great ballroom of London's newest — Hotel Treviles — all aglitter for our rock concert from Grizzly Glow with lead singer Scratchy Starshine and their number one on the charts, "Goetia" — no folks, that's not *Goats*, that's not old Coats, that's "Goetia" — Go-Ayeesha — the Great Go-go Mother Ayeesha, She Who Must Be Obeyed, hey; "Goetia" that has blasted to the top in just three days and threatens to outsell any side in history. I gotta professor here today, a genuine sixty-five carat professor — Clem Coward — and he's as they say an expert not just on rock *but* on the blackest of black magic too. Say, Clem, I hear from my man that these guys in the group — they're all Tantric initiates — that right?'

'Hang in there, Simon Sweet! This is that old black magic, a whole new scene. Man, these rites are taken from times even *before* black magic. But the new generation want something old now, it's time to get down and back to the prehistoric basics. It's the blackest and most backward that freaks them now, and these sing-songs they have — this Go-Ayeesha — are the oldest and freakiest, and make the old skeleton dance inside you. They're right into the primeval, sure. And that fills the chicks! The mommas, the groupies, even the teeny-boppers — it makes them *strong,* man, it's where the chicks were always at, the deep backward and abysm of the forest of first time.

'Names of all the demons for lyrics — is that how I read you, Clem? Show the viewers your eye, Professor, show them how the group had their surgeon open your third eye . . .'

The screen fills with Clem Coward's rather innocent, frowning face, crowned and fringed with flaming red hair — hence Simon Sweet's in-joke about sixty-four carats. The camera comes in past his gaze to the bridge of his nose, panning down on to his frown. As we watch, the brows go up, the tension relaxes that had concealed a small upright slit shaped like an almond standing on its end, like a caste-mark between his eyebrows. It is not just a mark, because with some manipulation of his facial muscles, Clem Coward causes the lips of this aperture to spread, and we see that it is actually a narrow entrance into his skull. The interior is red and moist, like a nostril, and a little grey snot oozes from it as we watch.

Click!

'This is a most solemn occasion. For the first time in the history of the world both European and Asian leaders are met in this great modern ballroom — the Cathedral Ballroom — of the Hotel Treviles, to discuss in the religious atmosphere appropriate to such a solemn — occasion the peaceful uses and non-proliferation of atomic energy.' The screen fills with the soaring imitation stone columns of a replica of Chartres Cathedral, down which the camera's eye travels. At the transepts many dignitaries are gathered in orderly patterns round a rostrum decorated with the flags of all nations, under each of which stands a clergyman in the appropriate garb of his religion, accompanied by an acolyte holding a sacred book or scroll.

'I can see the colourful orders and the vivid garments of the leaders of the smaller and perhaps more nervous nations contrasting with the confident sobriety, the grey flannel and dark clerical garb, of the stronger American and Russian delegates, and the serious uniforms of Red China.' Under the red flag are grouped two immaculately uniformed Chinese, each carrying a little red book. There is a sudden rustle of attention, and faces turn towards the vestry. An organ note sounds. There is applause. 'Ah . . . our Prime Minister, taking on Britain's ancient and established role as world mediator, has arrived to open the discussions . . .'

Click!

'Yeah, sure, that's what we're rapping with — they may be the names of demons — it all depends who you are, what you say are demons — but they may be the names of the animals — they may be the calls of animals, the love cries of the beasts that taught human beings to call out, and sing, and speak, as they lay awake in the tropical night, listening to the monkeys, in the hot dark cradle of the world — or they may be the sounds heard by the babies of these music-men when they were lying awake on hot summer nights listening to their parents quarrelling, and then making up their quarrel with orgasmic cries! Yeah, man, they must be love cries — why else would it sell?'

'Nudge, nudge, you've put your skinny finger right on the engine, Clem . . .'

'Dig it, man. The callings out of people as *they* dig each other written down and scored for rock, the rocking bedrock of what we really like to do! The mating-cries of animals written down and sung, as the keepers of those animals used to sing them to their goats, to keep them fertile, to their horses, to their great bulls, and watch the pizzles spring! You want to watch the pizzles dance? Then hear "Goetia"! The screwed-up oldies, those dry and dusty monks of the monasteries, they it was called these basic sounds, these lovely howls, demon-names. They warped those lovely sounds with their own hatred. But think of it like yoga-breathing, man. Like great gasps and guffaws doing your lungs good, clearing out all the pollution, getting you horny . . .'

'That would explain the mass revelry and scenes of wild enthusiasm that follow these guys about . . .'

'Far out, Simon! You're flying in a whole new firmament. It blows you away — it especially blows the birds away.'

Clem Coward's surgically-produced third eye is blowing enthusiastic spray like a surfacing whale's blow-hole.

'This is only one of the magic groups now operating on the media. I suppose it's our Grizzly Glow for the Groovy and that Geoffrey Glass Revivalist Group for the Gloomy . . . fighting for the souls of the younger generation . . .'

Click!

'With the arrival of the Prime Minister the delegates are now standing for the special ecumenical religious dedication of this extraordinary but timely conference. This unusual feature has been adopted with the unexpected acquiescence of both Russian and Chinese as a token of the desire of all present to stem the irresponsible tides of the occult now abroad in the world, especially among the young. And now here comes the popular Irish Archbishop, the Very Rev. Jack O'Metty, to the quadruple lectern accompanied by the Shinto Primate, the Dalai Lama, and his Reverence the Greek Orthodox Primate in England the Very Reverend F. Harry Stowe . . .'

The solemn procession arranged itself at the monstrous lectern. The effect of uniting in prayer is that not a single word can be heard of any of the four languages in which it is intoned. The screen splits, and shows us the four venerable faces, each deaf to everything beyond the sound of his own scriptures.

Click!

The two commentators are lounging in a control-room full of lighted screens that show from various angles the same scene that we can see through the glass picture-window beyond the console. Clem Coward is in full flight, mopping sweat and snot from his brow as he talks between bursts of humourless and contemptuous laughter. Simon Sweet, blond, in an off-white suit with a big check and narrow high shoulders, is quite subdued in contrast to Clem's high. The ornate salon on the screens and through the control-room window is filling up with fans of the group, mostly young girls dressed in the plain white flapping shirts over hairy tight sweaters and trousers that have become the uniform of followers of the lead singer, Scratchy Starshine, or Young Scratch as he is usually called. As Clem pauses in his expostulation for a moment, Simon reaches over and twists a knob, and the shrill and continuous sounds of chatter and excited anticipation blare out to us. Clem screws up this three eyes until Simon turns the sound control to 'quiet' again.

'Geoffrey Glass? That ass-faced darkie! Have you *heard* him? You know what they call him? Gee-Gee! Know what that comes from?'

'His followers say Gee-Gee affectionately to mean the possessed person, the horse that the spirits ride . . .'

'Naw . . . Shit . . . Gee-Gee stands for Girl Guide because of all the Girls he's Guiding . . .'

Click!

'Ladies and gentlemen, the Prime Minister of Great Britain.'

After the collapse of the Lib-Lab coalition in the late seventies, a former cabinet minister, now a Grand Old Man, grown in his retirement to Churchillian proportions — unfortunate this, since with his short stature obesity gave him the proportions of a perfect sphere — was brought back into active political life because of his great popularity. A certain inclination to show-biz made him the natural choice for chairman to this conference. The superpowers were glad to play along with this gesture of the UK for the reason that Britain was not only neutral ground, but also rapidly becoming the buffer-state on which any contained nuclear conflict, with clean weapons, would be fought out. Britain was becoming like Berlin in the fifties, a bone that the great dogs worried and chewed and used for territorial back-biting on a diminished uncommitting scale, like large-scale Monopoly. In this situation, like Berlin between the wars, the homeland of Shakespeare had become noted for its eccentricities and its cosmopolitan brothels. The tourist trade was very important, and was flourishing. Hotel Treviles, which covered the entire site of the cleared area formerly known as Soho, was noted for its orgy-suites that could be furnished in a trice as anything from a forest glade in a Tarzan film to an authentic-feeling parish church, with choirboys, or a public-school cricket-pavilion. The great ballrooms that were now occupied respectively by Grizzly Glow and their fans, and the Prime Minister and the world leaders with their echelons and escorts, were not basically as they now appeared, any more than a film studio is. They were large, square boxes, to the interiors of which had been fixed the veneer of a great Regency ballroom (as in a Scarlet Pimpernel film) and of Chartres Cathedral. They were booked to become the Forum in Rome and the Place du Tertre in three days' time.

The circular face of the Prime Minister of this extraordinary international scene filled the screen, and his nasal Mancunian voice began to weave its persuasive and confident spell.

'Messrs Chairmen, Mr President, Your Majesties, Your Imperial Highness, Your Reverences, Your Excellencies, Your Graces, My Lord Mayor . . .'

Click!

'You'll be very displeased, then, Professor Clem, to learn that this same Geoffrey Glass with his Disciples is also holding a meeting in this hotel.'

'So long as they keep from under the feet of the real people . . .'

Click!

'. . . in the conviction — I've said it before and I'll say it again — that today as never before we can settle the matter that has bedevilled our civilisation like Lucifer the Bearer of Light Brighter than a Thousand Suns, since that first day among the lizards and spiders of the Almogordo Desert that became no more than shadows fastened like the images of themselves to the photographic rock in that first great flash . . .' The anxious head of an aide pops into the picture and whispers to the Prime Minister. 'As I was saying, the first great question that confronts us today is, which one of them is God, and which one of them is the Devil?'

Click!

'Here we are, folks — at long last — MR STARSHINE WITH GRIZZLY GLOW IN "GOETIA, SONG OF THE ANGELS"!'

The sound knob is twisted on the screen and up come the welcoming howls of the rows of whiteshirted, shaggy-trousered, loose-haired girls that are packed into the beautiful Treviles ballroom. The rock group appear as at the end of a long tunnel of serried rows of people, through a camera sited in a balcony far up at the back of the hail, but the picture zooms in, like falling down a well lined with loose hair, to the platform where Grizzly Glow in their shaggier than shaggy clothes are solemnly pacing out an anticlockwise circle. The lead-guitar cries out like an elephant wounded in the throat, and the five young men, all of whom wear white single tusks projecting from their foreheads, like unicorns, leap to the microphones. The tallest of them, Young Scratch, who also wears what looks like a halo that is a black sun with writhing corona filaments of great brightness (but which everybody now knew was a projected hologram of a solar eclipse taken by a new process in Africa the year before), begins mouth-fondling his lyrics which are the names of demons.

'OSORRRRRRONOPHRIS JAPA JAPA JAPA SATAN-SATAT ARANIOS RHEIBERTFOR ATHELBESERKER A BLATHA SATATAT ABJEWEL THITASO IBIBIBIB ISISISISISISISIS THIAOW . . .'

Click!

The spherical speaking bladder of a face seems, by inlay technique, to be travelling rapidly down Chartres' dizzy aisles as it talks, but we are amazed and naughtily delighted to hear that the Treviles sound-proofing is not all it should be, or it has given way under the pressure of the acrid and excessive decibels of Grizzly Glow, and we can still hear the rock band even in this holy of holies of political deliberation, where all should be a reverent hush. The faint sound is here by distance only a pulse — we cannot hear voices — merely a discordant pulse. The Prime Minister can hear it too, though he wishes to pretend it does not exist, or that it is a beating within his own temples. In the tight and seamed leather of his football countenance, a slight furrow like the faintest of lace-holes has appeared between the eyes almost buried in their overhanging lids. He has begun to falter in his speech.

'. . . this great power that has been put into our hands and into our minds and indeed between our lips' — a startlingly-red tongue darts out and licks those lips. The effect is comparable to seeing a reptile's coils growing from a cherub's face. It is strange;

whether it is the television technique of superimposing realities, or the knowledge that Hotel Treviles is a cavern of illusions anyway, inside which Aladdin's hideaway these overdressed people are deciding all our fates, if we shall be burnt alive or no, or whether it is that Grizzly Glow's music clicked on and off is beginning to have a deeper effect than we expected (which, indeed, would be why the young girls dress up in their shaggy clothes like young goat-footed fauns to flock to it) — even the ordinary pictures on the respectable channel from now on seem to enlarge their suggestions, and their imagery seems to direct further insights, as when afterwards one could swear that this honest elder statesman's tongue, never before seen on television, was actually forked. Later events made this even more debatable, since the special effects appropriate to a rock concert appeared actually to *leak* between the channels. This forked tongue may have been the first sign.

'. . . and between the lips, hearts, minds and hands of every delegate here, especially not those in holy orders, since heavenly lightning is too serious a thing to be entrusted to the professionals, as someone, Lord Acton I think it was, always said, meaning no respect either to the clergy or soldiery, which can (as I was saying again as I've always said, and will say again) be the curse of mankind, that would, if we let it, clean the face of this smiling earth of all other Curses, and leave it shining like fused glass, a pearl of unwisdom' — and we do indeed now see that this is exactly how this man's face is shining, as it hurries by television through the airy columns which are its backdrop, rather like the suspended Godface of the Wizard of Oz, that old phoney surrounded by his quaking machines — 'or its redemption, that has proliferated like a noise, I mean a curse, which some make hay, I mean which some of us may say —' and in his old age, having lost some political tact, he snaps in an abrupt aside to that same aide: *'What is that bloody row?'*

Click!

The bloody row has gathered force, as a gale beating on the shore. The windy sounds have pounded the sea of faces and whirling hair into waves of rhythmic movement. It is the custom of the teenage followers of Grizzly Glow not only to dress in dazzling shirts that are worn loose over shaggy tights and jumpers, but at the concerts to set up a slow shaking of the head, so that the rhythm of the loose hair flows to and fro across the audience, like the spirallings and meanderings of a stream of water, though much much slower than that, of lava perhaps, flecked with all colours, predominantly dark with streaks of sharp blonde (like a melted ore of metal in the black molten rock), and there is one band of girls all of whom have dyed their hair a flame red, so that the lava has opened to let forth its gehennal fire. The music dictates this rhythm of the hair, and, at a slower wavelength, it is the custom to spread and flap once the tails of the white shirts in the hands, upwards, so that suddenly the dark and flecked sea of hair whitens in spindrift, as though the wind had caught it and flung it off in 'white horses'. And as these devotees testify, it is not long before a condition of trance is reached, and pictures, which are like the music made visible, flash into the mind, and are as quickly gone. To imitate this, a special technique has been devised, corresponding in its own way to the scenic elaborations on the staider channel. The producers of the programme have arranged that a film should run on their screen within the control-room that contains such abrupt and not altogether arbitrary images, and, according to their judgement of the climaxes of the music, should be flashed on the screens of the television audience, who have not the benefit of being present, and who could therefore probably not experience the trance directly. This is not cheating in any way, of course: the 'head-pix', as the interpolated film is called, are very carefully devised to be as realistic as possible according to the best modern techniques (as that which diverted us on the other channel when the Prime Minister's head was made to seem to be giving us a conducted visual tour of the *actual* Chartres Cathedral at the same time as he was delivering perhaps the most important speech of his career).

So that there shall be no doubt at all that this is being done, we are given frequent privy sights of the console, which shows on its numerous screens Grizzly Glow as seen through the camera lenses dotted about the hall in their various vantage-points; then a man with headphones says briskly, 'Run the head-pix,' and reverse numbers flash busily past on a proportion of those screens. Then we see a series of small pictures of ingenious special effects and documentary photographs that will be flashed fully on our screens at home in time, according to the producer's judgement, to the music, or when he considers that the normal viewer's span of attention is exhausted. This preview in the control-room is to reassure the viewer that the technique is about to be applied deliberately. The odd thing that was noticed at this time was that a sudden picture of an excessively realistic demon flashed for a moment on to our home-screens *before* the producer had called for his 'head-pix'. It was difficult to understand how this could have happened on a live programme. Had the occasion been on tape, then this image could have accidentally become spliced in. As it was, it was excessively tactless, since it showed, and on this rival channel, a body that was all face, and the face was the Prime Minister's, and it was covered with scales, and it did have a flickering forked tongue, but not a reptile's coils: rather it had eight scuttling spider-legs with which it travelled, our picture keeping pace with it, through crumbling columns of a wet substance that resembled columnar faeces, turds standing on their ends, and breaking up under their own weight. The Minister-Primespider was apparently running with a smiling face through these flowing unstable halls to escape the unspeakable terror of being drowned in filth. But it was all too quick to decide before Grizzly Glow, haloed in holograms of flickering fire, appeared once again, their drum-beats and howls never letting up for an instant.

Click!

'. . . the great sunstuff of the mushroom cloud that towers over our disunited nations which can, like Alice, nibble at one side and grow greater, or nibble the other and wink out as a wash of atomic particles . . . OSONOPHRIS . . .' The Prime Minister's face opens in a sudden sharp yelp: 'SATATAT A BLATHA.' The noise from Grizzly Glow has penetrated quite strongly into the facsimile of Chartres, and the Prime Minister appears to be one of the most sensitive there; he is responding already to the lyrics with his own calls. An aide's head appears on-screen, and we have a glimpse of hands easing the agitated speaker away from his microphone. The tactful camera moves to a general view of the delegates, who are presenting a frozen-faced appearance as it is evident that there is no sound-proofing against these modern sounds — yet how did they become so insistent, as though the walls themselves were broadcasting them?

Click!

The volume of the music is terrifying. The head-pix are now showing animals, leopards, running and pouncing on gazelles, knocking the fleet runners over and tearing the limbs from their haunches; a great grizzly bear hugging a pallid and bloody something which it carefully lets drop on the pine-needles, and then nuzzles; a shark swinging through the water and bending the bars of an aluminium cage, taking a mouthful of rubber-clad flesh from the diver within; a view of a vivisecting table; ants on a carcass; hair rippling across the stooping shoulders of the grizzly, ants stripping the meat off the white bones, the flash of teeth in the hairy muzzle of the grizzly, ants, grizzly-hair, girl-hair of audience, ants, grizzly, audience: the camera is insisting on the analogy between the great devouring organism of the antheap, the terrible engine of hairy destruction that is the grizzly, and the hair free-flowing and the white shirts flashing of the audience of young girls who are now calling out in rhythm to the time of the music their animal calls in response and in concert. Between the head-pix we see the tossing pelts of the composite animal of young girls that keeps changing its cries; then head-pix intervenes with an elephant fighting a tiger, the howdah lopsided and the great grey hide furrowed red by the tiger's claws, the elephant's rider hanging on for dear life; and there are cat-roars and trumpetings; hair flows in tide to the music; then in rhythm men are with clubs beating the brains out of baby seals, and there is a whimpering like the wet nappies of ten thousand babies. And always the fringes of the audience are advancing towards the stage in the live pictures, and at these fringes it is not white shirts that are swaying in time to the tossing of hair in undulating rhythms, it is the flickering of outstretched fingers and the flashing of polished nails among the hair and white shirts.

Click!

The frozen expression of the Archbishop of Canterbury. He

opens his mouth. 'ISCHUREYA. KOTHARATUS,' he says in conversational tones, 'ABROAOTH JOELLISSI SATATAT.'

Click!

'ABRASAR BARRIO JOELLISSI CHINKMAT SABRIAN ANANIAS THOT MARCHLION ABAOOTH MIGHTY AND FORMLESS ONES,' howl Grizzly Glow to their transported audience.

Now all the hands are stretched out and flickering like fire, like electric current, and there is a movement in the mass of girls in the sea of tossing hair that is gathering into one island or raft the flecks and islets of hair that is red, and the possessors of this coloured hair having been collected in the centre of the audience are now being extruded towards the platform where Grizzly Glow are congratulating themselves on their potent song. They have had to turn up their amps — we see the guitarist fiddling with the equipment — to hold their own with the animal noise of the enthusiastic crowd they face. Young Scratch is having a little trouble with his nose; he wafts his hand in front of it as though there is a sudden rank smell that is too much for him, for he sways, and then claps that hand to that nose for it has suddenly begun to spurt blood — the excitement is too much — and as his nosebleed gushes on to his white makeup there is a howl of renewed and extreme frenzy from the audience, which now ejects its red-haired members, who leap up on to the stage and seize their stars, lift them up and throw them into the sea of hair, where hands are ready to receive them. Our camera shows us Young Scratch's face flying through the air, bleeding copiously from the nose, before he disappears among the white shirts and black tresses. For a moment we are not sure whether this vision of the flying bleeding head is another head-pic, as the sensitive machine now inserts on to our screens visions of earthquakes with bodies crushed, flooding rivers with whole townships carried away, and a lava flow from an erupting volcano descending upon and consuming a manger of animals among which a woman has given birth.

Click!

The immobile faces of the delegates have turned sharply towards the west doors of the cathedral, for a new note has entered the interfering noise. All there except the English party have heard that noise before, and fear it; it is the sound of a rioting mob.

Click!

There are no signs of the group. Their instruments and equipment are now being thrown by the mob to the mob, who are using them to attack the tapestry-covered walls and the elegant wood-veneered plastic furniture and the fibreglass pillars of their simulated ballroom. As the plugs come out of the electrical equipment, and as their fuses blow, what little melody there was in the group's music disappears from the sound that pours from the room, but the beat is still there, and the volume is not diminished.

Click!

The BBC commentator stares seriously out of the picture, then his body begins to dance violently like a shaken puppet. His serious, confiding, hushed commentator's face does not betray this event by a flicker.

Click!

The salon is denuded of furniture and false walls. It is a large bare plastic room with a mob twisting and turning across its floor. Young Scratch appears held high in the air on the women's multiple arms, his mouth wide as though he were still singing, his eyes bulging. A clawed finger slips below the lid of one eye and levers it out on its string. A rapid succession of head-pix shows us butchers splitting animals in an abattoir and blood running like a fast stream through gutters. We resume a close-up of Scratch's mutilated face, which slowly turns upside down, and then drops loosely out of the picture, for it has been torn from the body. A group of young women have formed a rugby scrum with the head, and are busy hooking at it below linked bodies. A long-haired scrum-half waits for the trophy to emerge from the kicking legs.

Click!

The Greek Orthodox Primate, whose rigid black head-dress and full beard betray no emotion, whose lips are pursed so that no untoward names should spring from his lips, thrusts out a cross and waves it slowly at the nonplussed delegates.

Click!

Two simultaneous movements are taking place in the salon that has been stripped to its bones. The mob has noticed the BBC control-room window. It is attacking the tough glass with microphone stands. We see the figures of Professor Clem and Simon cowering inside. A rapid switch of cameras shows us their backs and through the glass a sea of hair and hands swaying like aggressive seaweed in an aquarium. A sudden clang-and-clatter shatters the glass, which falls free. Now our collective eye has skipped to the camera in the main room, which shows us the two commentators being slowly dragged over the jagged glass and given to the main mob. Head-pix shows us Gulliver cramming into a mouth of blood Lilliputian people of all classes and colours.

The second movement occurs as the great doors of the room burst open, and show a line of police with drawn truncheons advancing towards the women. The police have linked arms, and look very white-faced. There is a new sound in the room among the animal calls and the fast-fading memories of the beat of Grizzly Glow's song; it is a sudden gleeful laughter as the police appear, and a high note of exultation which we realise means 'They have let us out of this room!' and there is a great hotel full of people beyond these puny police, who are now swept aside by a concerted rush. In a moment, the rock salon is empty, except for stains, broken scenery, and a good deal of litter of vile bundles, and stains on to which our camera, impelled by some automatic instinct of the mechanism (for surely no cameraman has survived here) inconsiderately begins to pan to close-up on a policeman's helmet rocking on its side on the floor, still full of the policeman's moustached face. Head-pix appears to have taken matters into its own hands and now intervenes with a man playing a violin to some people at a restaurant, and a tropical beach with undulant hula-dancers after: it has begun to think soothing pictures, whether with a belated desire to tranquillise, or an ironic intention, we do not know, not at first, not until we receive the next picture, which is of the blind violinist in the forest playing to the murderous Frankenstein monster, in Boris Karloff's impersonation, and the monster crushes a china girl-doll in one great hand as the music rises to gipsy crescendo.

Click!

The concourse of delegates remains petrified. The golden Greek cross is still suspended in the hands of the Orthodox Primate. The delegates are all ears. Head-pix has infiltrated into this channel, for we see a herd of okapi, perhaps two thousand of them, with ears pricked and on each animal a hoof poised, ready to flee. The delegates reappear, and now we can hear what they can hear, animal noises given in a rhythmic beat, as before, yes, but now something more terrifying: the pounding of feet shod as with hooves as a mob of two thousand maenads runs through the corridors of the Hotel Treviles towards these innocent world leaders in Chartres Cathedral. The sound as it mounts is hypnotic, like the stampede of the herd of buffalo that head-pix now throws across the screen. The buffalo gallop across the screen and leave, by an inlay process, the delegates standing in the buffalo plain as the dust settles. Now they are again in the cathedral: there is no escape by television. No escape at all. With a thunderous clap the great west doors spring open and shake the fabric as they strike the walls. In surges enters the howling, trumpeting, cackling, roaring maenad rout, a terrible swirling picture of hair and nails and bloody shirts. Head-pix responds with the close-up of the jaws of a spider sucking at the collapsing body of a fly. By an inlay process head-pix shows the delegates hanging suspended in that web. The spider, with a great crackling of harness, picks its way towards them. Head-pix clears to show the reality: a torrent of women with murder in every fibre of their bodies rushing down the nave of Chartres towards the chancel in which the world leaders are gathered. The whole world is watching this scene. Fingers in vast military complexes are fumbling with the coded keys that will design and compute and recompute the strategies of successive alerts. Will the rout reach and dismember the American President first, or the Russian Chairman, and in that case does this constitute an act of war? All over the world the murderous silos glide open, while the women of murder run howling down the cathedral aisle. The howling takes on the beat and rhythm 'WAA wa WAAAAAA wa WAAAA Wa' as the moment of destruction of the hated world as we know it nears. So that neither we nor the delegates may mistake the mob's purpose, the front rank are carrying and waving pieces of the dismembered rock band.

It is doubtful whether the delegates truly realised the terrible fate in store for them as they stood, without protocol for this event, waiting for their security men to take it away again. The security men were aware of what had happened, naturally, since the whole event had been monitored on their television screens, but the events had happened so strangely and swiftly that none of the senior men had been able to come to a decision. The intervention of head-pix had not aided their composure or grasp of reality.

Suddenly a tall black man stepped from a sidechapel full into the path of the running women. His nostrils were distended, his head thrust forward, his eyes glaring and his brows drawn down. He opened his mouth and white light blared on our screens, in the manner in which they became overloaded when the cameras are pointed at, say, an atomic flash, and then the picture of the mushroom cloud forms again as the screens clear. White noise came out of the speakers: a violent hiss, called white because it contains all sounds, as white light contains all colours. The screen cleared and the echoes of his voice were rolling round the plastic aisles. 'BE STILL! BE STILL!'

The women had stopped running. Now that they were still, one could see clearly the dreadful objects they held in their hands and with which they had decked themselves. One tall girl was swathed from head to foot in grey-green intestine, which glittered as she swayed and panted. Small pieces of shit dropped from a free-swinging end near her feet. Another woman had a small fleshy object gripped in her white teeth, like a cat carrying a small tan kitten, and it was not so bad, this one, until you saw that the object was a man's genitals. Another girl, in the front of the rioters, had made a kind of slapstick with a microphone stand and some spongy material, which looked like lungs. The women were dreadfully bespattered with blood, and their clothes were rent: the upper garments, for the main part, the breasts showing through the loose hair, the trousers simulating furry legs still intact, except where many women had clawed the cloth to expose the pubis. The cameras — manned by stalwart technicians who calmly considered this the biggest story of all time — gave us close-ups of these women standing still, in the tension of whether they would or would not over-run the black man who stood in their path, behind him the world leaders who had seemed no serious obstacle, vulnerable in their cathedral. A few khaki uniforms had now become visible and a last stand looked possible if Glass failed — but who wanted to be seen on television ordering the gunning-down of women with machine-pistols? To show that head-pix would be as obstructive as possible to any such procedure, head-pix now showed some quick flashes of just that kind of event from newsreels: Jewish women clutching their babies stood on the lip of a trench and were mown down into it by soldiers among barbed wire and concentration camp watch-towers.

The screen cleared again to show Glass, still with his head thrust forward. Again his mouth opened, and white light filled the screen, white noise the speakers, like the roar of a waterfall. When the pictures returned Glass confronted in that cathedral aisle not women, but three massive boulders that struck each other in turn, sliding behind each other and taking up a new position of collision, striking each other again with showers of sparks which crackled also like interference on our screens. It was like the stones of Avebury or Stonehenge dancing, as they are said to do on certain nights of the year. Glass walked towards them, aiming, it seemed, at their momentary arches and portals which they then destroyed by a massive sliding and clocking together, while Glass slowly trod as though he knew the way, and the correct moment. He found that moment, and passed safely between one boulder and another in the instant before he would have been crushed, in a shower of sparks.

Beyond the rocks, which as Glass passed them disappeared, there are no women. The aisle is empty. Across it, however, has risen a great wall, as though the outside of the cathedral has become the inside, and it has raised its massive stones and buttresses within itself, high as its inner roof. The wall is composed of these great blocks, and carved flutings rising to corbels that meet the ceiling solidly. Out of a side-chapel steps a great dog with bared teeth, a pregnant bitch, with belly full and studded with tits. Her growling fills the screen with jagged flashes. Glass walks slowly onwards. The dog is as large as he would have been on all-fours, and now we see this as with an easy motion he gets down on his hands and knees lightly, and with the stride of an animal lopes towards the bitch. She snarls jaggedly, he responds with yelps that fill the screen with whiteness; as the picture clears we see him disengaging himself from the dog, with which he has just coupled. Now he walks on his two legs towards the wall, and as he comes to it he puts his shoulder to it and pushes his way through.

On the other side of the wall it is as though we are under the sea. There is a ripple on the screen, with which television drama-makers commonly depict this situation, and the groining of the cathedral walls is festooned with weeds and corals, which wave slowly in the currents. A great three-masted wooden ship is sunk on the oozy floor in the background, gold pouring from its split sides. Many fish swim in the water, turning their coloured bodies suddenly from edge-on to full profile, astonishing the camera with the sudden appearance of rainbow flocks.

Squatting in front of the ship on a cluster of boulders in chiaroscuro resembling Leonardo's picture of the Virgin of the Rocks, is a strange assembly. An octopus sits on one rock like a wise dome with legs and heavy-lidded eyes, slowly pulsing its hollow body. On another rock sits a similar dome, but made of jelly, and transparent; in the jelly inclusions, patterns of glands and canals; and crowned with a ring of tentacles. Seated on the middle rock is a hideous drowned body.

Fragments of the body peel off in the currents, so that it is surrounded by a swirl of flakes, like dandruff flurried in the water. The skin has swollen and its layers split apart, soggy as soaked cardboard; a flap on the belly is coming off, and flops lazily. The legs, which are pushed out as though to prop the body on the rock, are like swollen sausages, in two sets of two links. The feet are skeletal, and a flock of little fish are nibbling at them. The torso is swollen into an hourglass bladder without features, without nipples or navel, nothing but an immense swelling that is disintegrating its skin into the water, where the fish feed on what its decay makes. On top of this immense dome is a skeleton head, tiny in proportion, with the skin not swollen on it, but shrunken and tight. Eyes still lurk in the cavernous sockets, the teeth gleam, and long black hair floats and sways rhythmically in the currents. This hair is much involved with corals and small shelly creatures which have fastened on it as their homes; thick and matted with sand, it flows towards the walls and is knitted in with the weeds that trail down them. The effect is of an immense soaked cottage loaf of bread, with legs, on top of which sits this tiny skull with long hair.

A tiny skull which talks, and moans, and raises its voice to be heard when the currents veil its face with its own ever-growing hair. The nails coil from hands which are simply fat pads, and stand like two large spiral shells at each side of the figure, each wound out of five strips of fingernail, and rooting deep and immobile in the ooze.

As the skull talks, we can sometimes hear its words, and sometimes the words become pictures of the words on our screens. It is saying that men's sins (and here we have more newsreel pictures of tanks lurching up beaches and men jerking in the orgasms of death beneath their caterpillar tracks) have made her ill, and her hair hangs over her face and is matted and slovenly because of men's sins, and it is these which have drowned her and made her body putrescent so that it poisons the water (and now we see cornfields desolated by atomic catastrophe; the good food catching fire in flamethrower-bursts) and the water is that which travels through the world creating living forms, powered by the sun and the moon, making its imitative magic of its spiralling form on the earth's surface, fish that are shaped like water, shells that are shaped like water, as though water slowed itself to make life in forms which are like water passing through water in the embryo of the human being, in the two great spiralling hemispheres of the human brain, like agitated water. But the water is poisoned, is poisoned, moans the skull, and the hair that pours from my head which is the water of the world is poisoned too, so all is poisoned, moans the corpse.

Glass walks slowly forward underwater and reaches up and takes the corpse of the goddess by her shoulder (and the skin separates in a shower of flakes as his fingers sink into it), and with his other hand, the fingers outspread, begins combing the terrible hair, for her fingers cannot do this for herself. As he combs, the lines of flow of the hair begin to come free, and there is a squeaking and grating from the filth in the hair. His hand becomes clotted with it, and he throws it free into the water, where fish like coloured birds dart in and snap it up, his hand then returning to his patient combing. Now the screen flashes with these squeaks and soft tearing, now it clears to show the women walking round in a circle that weaves in a complex shape among the pillars of the cathedral, and Glass is walking with them, his head bent, and tears streaming down his face. Gradually this pacing procession nears the world leaders, who join the line and walk with heads bowed, one by one.

I found my own cheeks wet. The screen suddenly went blank. All transmissions were finished for the time being.

It is recounted of Albert Einstein that, as a schoolboy, he diverted himself with fantasies in which he travelled as fast as a beam of light. As he did so, the electromagnetic vibration, the very stuff of the universe, slowed down, relatively to his own speed, and became a solid thing, undulant with its vibrations. Einstein's visualisation of this was so strong and the fantasy so beautiful that, it is said, the young boy came to ejaculation by imagining himself riding astride this beautiful thing, like a boy on an infinite leaping dolphin. However that may be, such imaginings were the start of the theory of relativity, the consequence of which is our modern world of nuclear power and anguished brinkmanship. In television we have, like Einstein, slowed down or shortened radio waves so that they become visible pictures of solid things. We have lived for many years in this artificial environment of shaped radio waves, but before this we have lived for all time in an environment of radiation from the sun and the stars, modulated by the presence and circuits of the moon and the planets, the slowing down of which into solid objects and visible pictures has become our teeming life on earth. What the cosmic machinery did to create our bodies and minds, we have imitated by our television broadcasts. But now it has happened that these ancient cosmic patterns have in a strange way been interpreted to us on television, have modulated with these pictures and these sounds of the man called Glass, the triggers of a movement towards self-discovery that has permanently altered humankind. As these patterns have become television, so, it appears, has the nature of television altered. As the electro-magnetic radiation of the sun (only a small proportion of which is its glorious visible light) moved the water and the rains and fertilised the teeming earth, so the patterns of waves of these television broadcasts have now acted. As, it is said, the vibration of the Angel Gabriel's voice (by permission of the Father in the sky) made the Virgin Mary virginally pregnant, so it has come to pass that the whole world, soaked through and through by the actions of Glass on television, responded thus in its deepest fibres. And fifty per cent of those who had watched the colour pictures of his triumph, both men and women, found, in a short three months, that they had become pregnant.

Chapter 7

Mr Glass is in one of the star dressing-rooms beneath the stage of the Albert Hall. He sits at a dressing-table with its glaring bulbs, in front of the hinged mirror that multiplies his reflections into infinity. His party are going to examine him tonight, and he has been called to a public confession of his sins, People's Republic style. Canon John and Sylvia Pendennis have, between them, unearthed the records of his trial, now nineteen years old, and they have placed them in the hands of the committee. Glass must now make public confession before a representative four thousand initiates of the religion — or is it a science? — of which he has been the leader. 'But I am not the leader,' he protests to his shocked and solemn committee, 'I am simply the Petar, the show-er. I am merely a man who acquired the ability to respond to what is happening in the deep nature of our sisters and brothers! To respond, and to show. . .'

'But you have been in prison.'

'Yes, I was given *life* . . .'

'You have been imprisoned for one of the cruellest crimes ever recorded in a civilised community!'

The situation is very much complicated by the event of the mysterious pregnancies. Of the committee of sixteen people sitting behind the great table, four of the women are in an advanced state of pregnancy, including Sylvia, but also four of the men are carrying on their fronts bulges which to them seem to rival the swelling dome of the Albert Hall itself. They have been assured by doctors, by the finest gynaecologists, that each bulge contains a fully-formed human being, perfect to the last detail, except perhaps for the last-minute touches such as the tiny toenails, and ready to be born. The doctors were very much stimulated by this phenomenon. It was rumoured in Islam that Mohammed would be born again in a Second Coming from a man: English soldiers serving in the Middle East used to say that this was the reason why Mussulmen wore baggy trousers: to conceal their possible pregnancies, to affirm the possibility — or to conceal the actual lack. Round the table we can see this: baggy trousers have come into fashion. Canon John does not need to wear them: he has merely taken out his cassock, a kind of frock already, so that his bulge is not obtrusive. A second male committee-member, who is also one of the executive council of Gay Liberation, has used every expedient to emphasise the forthcoming happy event by wearing snug satin trousers and a smock-like shirt. The other men are all wearing baggy trousers: but you can easily see which two are actually pregnant, thinks Glass gloomily. They are against him, the male mothers, not the least because of this. The doctors say that an enormous and unprecedented enlargement of the prostate, or *uterus masculinus*, has taken place, though without the pain or disease that is the usual accompaniment to much smaller prostate changes in late middle age. There was a theory that this occurred in men who had suppressed their natural femininity all through their lives. Participation in the Rites of Glass (as the showings are now called) apparently causes a slight enlargement of this organ immediately. In the male pregnancies a re-routing of the urine-carrying urethral tube occurs, so that it passes between two lobes of the foetal envelope. There is, however, no external aperture for the delivery, so in the case of the pregnant men it is expected that caesarian section will be inevitable. Now that everybody's time is so close, medical teams are on emergency stand-by round the clock.

But the pregnancies have complicated the situation with regard to Glass. Now that so many leaders of the Groups have been trained, Glass might simply have been dismissed from the movement, forcibly retired with as little fuss as possible. But his practices have brought about a new kind of situation: not mass conversions, merely, not mass possessions and rising 'goodlier than before' alone, but mass pregnancies. The urgent question is, is Glass the true father of these children?

If he is, then clearly he cannot be dismissed! If he is the Father of this new generation of brothers and sisters (assuming that they are born safely) then he is needed, and will be needed by all the unmarried mothers, male and female, that are carrying his children. There will have to be mass weddings with the black man, perhaps by radio broadcast, so that the half of humanity that is pregnant by Glass's television broadcast can be made honest men and women, as the old phrase used to be. More important, it would weld the people concerned into a church the intimacy and power of which had never before been seen in human history.

Of course, the scientists were full of probable explanations, but no certain facts had been gleaned so far. There had been something about that broadcast that had caused a series of mysterious events in the deep physiology of both the men and the women concerned. It had been known for generations that if you placed a sea-urchin egg in a different concentration of seawater stronger than the one that it was accustomed to, or if you pricked a frog's egg with a glass fibre, then the eggs would start to divide and grow as if they had been penetrated by a sperm in the normal manner of fatherhood. In due course a sea-urchin or a frog grew from this fatherless egg, and you had an animal conceived and grown parthenogenetically: literally, by virgin birth. It was the myth of many religions that the Father in Heaven begot and caused himself to be born of a Virgin; it was included in the myth of the Christian Church, hitherto the most powerful on the face of the earth. But now it had happened to millions of people. There was a great fear in many quarters that the babies would be black.

For undoubtedly Glass was as much the father as the Father in Heaven, the Word spoken by the angel to the Virgin Mary, was the father of Jesus. The scientists might say that a particular concentration and shape and modulation of colour television radio waves had caused a cell to separate from the ovaries of the women and in the prostates of the men, just as a sonic beam could detach cells if directed at the same organs (and they had tried all this with animals), and this same modulation of patterns had caused the said cells to begin to divide and embed, producing all the effects of a normal pregnancy, including development of the mammary glands of the men (many of whom had taken to wearing beards also, to assert their continued masculinity even in this pass). But just as these radio waves, caught on an aerial and interpreted by a television set, produced images of Glass's actions and Glass's triumph, so, it was argued, if caught in the womb of a woman or the prostate of a man, and interpreted by their sensitive DNA material, the images that would be produced would be those of Glass, and therefore Glass was the Father, reproduced in radio by his own image. All this was highly speculative and theological, though it was argued powerfully by the pro-Glass party, but it was soon taken out of the realm of conjecture by a scientific experiment. The experiment had to be done, since it was likely to be argued by the courts that if Grizzly Glow were the fathers, and not Glass, or if other people appearing on the television broadcast, such as the Prime Minister or the American President, or the Roman Catholic cardinal who had been glimpsed briefly, were the fathers, then there would be important rights of succession and inheritance to settle. The people most concerned about this were the heirs and estate of Grizzly Glow, since the rock group had died owning millions.

So scientists played the tele-recording of the whole broadcast in the laboratory to patient animals: they did not even show the poor creatures the pictures, merely subjected them to the whole half-hour wash of waves. Sure enough, the rabbits and the mice became pregnant and delivered healthy offspring. Then they played only a part of the broadcast to the animals: the part where Grizzly Glow were performing their music before the catastrophe. The animals developed enormous cancerous tumours. When the Prime Minister's speech was played to them in the form of these radio waves, no conception occured at all. The bellowing of the maenads was played: the animals were born with St Vitus dance. Clem Coward and Simon's cross-talk act was played: the animals were born without faces. The solemn announcer of the atomic conference was played: the animals were born with ankylosed spines, welded into one rigid, unbending unit, and soon died.

When the broadcast and the sequence of events were played entire, the offspring were normal. They were particularly healthy when only the image of Glass alone was played to them, held still in one modulated wave repeating and repeating, such as when the action is seen frozen on a television set. The animals were most fecund when Glass was played to them as he stroked the terrible hair of the drowned goddess.

The conclusion of these experiments was that it was undoubtedly the images and actions of Glass that caused these pregnancies. The heirs of Grizzly Glow pressed for a decision in the probate courts, and the learned judges ruled that Glass was lawfully the Father of the children, except in those cases where it could be proved otherwise. (Pregnancies could have occurred on that spectacular night by other means. As one learned counsel quipped: 'My wife and I always copulate on all fours.' Learned judge: 'Why is that so?' Counsel: 'How else could we watch television, m'lud?')

This meant that the Glass committee could not discard Glass. But his crime was a particularly sadistic one, and though he had expiated it in the eyes of society, he must also expiate it in the eyes of those people who had first responded to his powers, and still took him as their example and leader, though he had always protested that he was nothing more than a responder, a reflector of the people he encountered, and it was his privilege and his grace to receive those impressions which he returned in the form that he had found to be effective. 'And how did you find this form,' asked Canon John, frowning terribly, for the hormones of his pregnancy had grown him enormous black eyebrows; 'how did you find this power?'

'I found it in prison,' said Geoffrey Glass, 'when I was shut away and had to study by myself.'

'What subject then did you study?' enquired John, condescendingly.

'My crime,' said Glass, his fingers tapping on the polished table; 'it was my crime that gave me my knowledge. And my knowledge is no more than how to reflect. In prison I learnt to reflect . . .'

'We can all reflect,' said John.

'It's not that easy,' said Glass. 'You have to have something that won't go away to reflect about, like a crime.'

'Like what you did.'

'Yes, said Glass, 'that was so terrible that I had to reflect it deeply, for I could not forget what I had done.'

'Have you forgotten now?'

'No.'

'It is with you in this instant.'

'Yes.'

'It is ever-present?'

'Yes.'

'Present everywhere?'

'Yes.'

'Then it must conceal God from you, who is also eternal and omnipresent.'

'My crime made God.'

'You created God?'

'I thought I had created a crime, and then I found that I had stripped the veil away from God.'

The committee's decision was that Glass must face, in person, as many initiates as possible. Television broadcasts were now banned, until their effects on the populace could be studied, but sound-broadcasts were apparently quite safe, so any meeting could be made public, and justice heard to be done. Glass had to make public confession, and the reaction of his initiates would determine his innocence or his guilt, whether his crime was to be valued or rejected. If rejected, it would be, everybody thought, rejected by the most cruel means, since the mob would undoubtedly become possessed during the meeting, and, should he lose his power over them, then Geoffrey Glass himself would be torn to pieces, like so many others before him.

* * *

And now Glass sat in the dressing-room of the Albert Hall while the great beehive above him filled with his disciples, some against him, some for him, but few so far knowing the facts. He had to tell them. Glass sat in front of the triple mirror, his reflection multiplied by its wings over and over, just as his image would be multiplied in the wombs of half the people on earth, down the corridor of generations, to infinity. For as long as humanity lasted, there would be few people in whose veins Glass's image did not flow.

As he watched in the mirror, his fingers began to tap out a little drum-tune: 'SATATA SATATA SATATATABLE SATATAT SATATATABLE.' Then the wings of the mirror on either side filled up with other images than himself. On his right hand Sylvia Pendennis appeared, her monkey-face looking severe and yet compassionate, tiny above her great body, for his crime revolted her, and had from the first hearings of his trial, which she had attended: it had determined the course of her life and the abandoning of her profession; yet she was carrying his child, and what she was about to learn from its father must surely again determine the course of a life, her behaviour and attitude to the child made of Glass. On his left hand Canon John appeared, his great black brows overhanging his lean clean-shaved cheeks giving him a ferocity of countenance which suited his terrier-like persecution of Glass and the uncovering of the records, together with the manipulation of the committee that had eventually indicted their beloved leader: his face now spoke his role of inquisitor. Yet he too was carrying this man's child, and what he learnt must inevitably change him and his attitude to the pregnancy: was it a monstrous conception forced upon him, bearing monsters; or was it the opening up in this religious man of his deepest femininity in its aspect of Creatrix? Would he now know the emotions of Mother God, unlike the myriads of black-clothed priests of the Church before him? None so far had been compelled to hide their pregnancies in loose frocks, John thought wryly, except Pope Joan. How would this Glass get out of the trap that he, like Judas, had set him? Would it force his hand, to declare Messianic power? Would he go down, be torn and consumed in the great riot of four thousand people rushing down on to the stage of the Albert Hall? His body would become bloody dust, human mince, and would nowhere be found. Or would this be his crucifixion and not his deletion? Would he like Another rise again? Double-Judas, male and female Judas, both carrying the child of his teaching, had brought him to this point, and were filled with these thoughts, as Glass rose and turned from the mirror to be taken by them into the hall.

Chapter 8

'I killed a man, very horribly, and was given life.'

Mr Glass was a tiny black figure on an immense platform draped in white by the management of the Albert Hall, who considered such a stage-dressing suitable for religious meetings. At the back of the platform was fixed a very large placard that soared up so far and so wide that it very nearly concealed the tallest pipes of the famous organ. On this placard was painted the emblem that the Society of Glass had recently adopted: a red Tau cross like a letter T with a red serpent entwined there like a letter S. This represented the famous sat-a-tat-tat of the mouth that heralded a possession. Initiates when they approached this state were found to breathe out with a hissing sound ssssssssssss, and then as the muscles of the jaw went lax it jumped or rapped to this breath, making the syllable SATATAT. This sound had first been interpreted as a 'demon-name'; now it was a technique for producing the state. By chanting 'SATATATSATATAT SATATA TATAT SSSSSATATATA' and whirling round, the experienced initiate could produce an initial state of dissociation, into which his greater powers rushed, and his eventual harmony was signalled by the bee-hum.

'I killed a man, very horribly, and was given *life!*'

The immense audience, which had been deathly still, rustled. The hall was full, the four thousand seats occupied. There was a quality of attention in the air which the great auditorium, the great hive-shaped dome lined with galleries, and the galleries lined with seats, had rarely known. The seats curved round in the great circular space, seeming to hang suspended in the slight haze that had already gathered under the towering roof. Half the people there were in the latter stages of pregnancy, so Glass's audience consisted of the unborn as well as the born.

'I served eighteen years of my sentence, and after that came to live in the village where the Plague of Witches first began, and where our Society began. It was here that I encountered Sister Pendennis and Brother John Cuttance. These were the roots of our Society. You are its branches, leaves and fruit.'

There is a sigh throughout the hall, like a breath through a cavern, or through a tree-head of leaves. Glass faces the tapestry of white faces and colourful clothes. He himself is dressed in a black loose jacket, with an open white shirt. As he contemplates all these individuals, poised along the walls of the great dome, spread like a carpet in the circular arena at his feet, he knows that all these separate and distinct persons could become one beast, that would throw itself upon him and devour him without noticing the meal.

'During the eighteen years of my confinement I learnt something you now all know.'

In front of Glass, carrying the lectern and microphones, is a broad, wide, dark, and highly-polished table. He moves away from the microphones, pulls out a chair, and sits at this table. With his fingers he taps out drum-beats on the wood. His voice can he plainly heard, though he has moved away from the microphones. It grows savage and wild, and mocks in parody his own accent.

'I learnt this little song, this little tune. MISTUH GLASS SATATATABLE — MISTUH GLASS SATATATABLE — MUSTUH GLASS SATATATABLE — AH SATATATABLE BAAS — FUH EIGHTEEN WHOLE YEARS AH SATATABLE ALL BY MAHSELF — HONEYCHILE — ALL ON HIS OWNSOME IN HIS GLASS HONEYCELL MISTUH GLASS SATATATABLE YESSUH! — SATATAT — SATATAT — SATATAT — SATATATABLE . . .'

As he speaks the chant, a murmur of response comes from many throats. 'SATATAT SATATAT' picks up a deep chord within them, and unless he is careful, thinks Canon John, who is sitting with others of the committee in the front row, he will have a mass possession and tearing before he has even started to tell his story! John now wonders how the committee will fare in that case, if they are, like himself, not initiates of possession, preferring prayer. The sardonic bishop and the wool-headed one, sitting with him in the row, would fare as badly, he thought grimly. But it is as though with skill Glass has thrown a few ripples through the audience's sensitivity, to remind them of how they have been swayed, and why they are here, and he has now let these impulses subside, for he goes on with a sudden gentling of voice.

'That was my little chant. It was my song. The small thing that came into my mind the moment I was sentenced, and the small thing that came true and which filled my mind (as you fill this hall) for nearly two decades of solitary confinement. . .'

And now his voice rises to a scream and his hand pounds on the table and the audience screams back at him:

'MISTUH GLASS SATATATABLE — MISTUH GLASS SATATATABLE — MISTUH GLASS SATATATABLE!'

And the great bass scream, lowered in pitch by the size of the building, rolls round the dome like thunder. All seem to listen to the dying away of that thunder, and Glass's voice comes small and still after it.

'Why, this small thing, this mere word, after the first ten years of repeating it once every three seconds throughout the day and most of the night and in my sleep, one hundred and five million, one hundred and twenty thousand times, why, it had grown so solid like the wooden table in the prison cell in which I sat, tapping out its tune, that I placed my two hands flat on my song, and I felt out its grain, and I put my shoulder to my song, and it swung aside like the hinged door it was, and I saw my TABLE at which I sat for the first time and I saw the MAN who sat at that table for the first time, and I saw that TABLE and MAN sing together. You all of you know that song. It has the sound of bees.'

A deep hum resounded for an instant round the dome, from left to right, as though the people to one side started it and uttered it for a split second, and the people next to them followed and passed it on, but it only had time to go round once, since Glass was speaking of it again.

'My table was singing aloud with the simplest truths, as I sang. It was a table of wood, and sitting at it was a black man who was by accident no table of wood, but he was made of the same earth as that wood had grown from, and the wood was there before him, and he had evolved under the shelter of that tree, feeding on its fruits and on the flesh that also sheltered in that leafy wood, and in this table you could see the flow of the universe that had paused for a moment to become a tree, you could see the grain of it like the sculptor's fingerprint, and it was the same grain that paused a short instant when water splashed — and look, it is here written, the real presence.'

Glass seized the carafe of water that stood on the table, and upended it so that water flowered and flowed across the wood towards them.

'. . . or that paused for a slightly longer time to become the pattern of black man that is sitting here and the people who are listening to him contained in a great shape round as the bellies of many of you within which the audience of cells that is your child, listens to you . . . I looked into that table and saw its song and I looked into that black man and saw that the universe within him was singing too.'

The bee-hum is passing round the hall like the circling flight of insects, gathering momentum and volume as it does so, and Geoffrey Glass abruptly rises to his feet and the hum dies away.

'But the doorway to this moment when my skin became my deep glass was the doorway that was the table and the song of the table SATATAT SATATAT and the doorway to my table was a door of steel that was the door to my cell and the door to MAH HONEY-CELL was the great studded doorway of the gates of the prison and the doorway to these gates was the DOUBLE DOUBLE DOUBLE doors of the prison van plying to and fro on its business of transporting black meat from the prison to the courtroom and from the courtroom to the prison during the one hundred and sixty-three days of my famous trial which the world has forgotten and allowed to fall into its silence, down, down, down into the silence and the emptiness that is full of life, like the great rearing abyss of this hall as you listen to me without sound.

'Sitting in the courtroom was the doorway to my imprisonment and he was dressed in red and white and black and he was the JUDGE.'

Glass's voice becomes an exact reflection of that courtroom scene so long ago. His mouth opens, and out of it comes the rapping of a gavel, and the sounds of a room of people settling down, and a sniffling bony voice that says:

'The prisoner will stand . . . . Geoffrey Glass, you have been convicted of an abominable crime, for which I can find no excuse in circumstance or nature.'

The accusation echoes, and Glass allows the echo to die away, before he resumes softly:

'And the doorway to the judge was — the ABOMINABLE CRIME.' The judge's phrase echoes in the judge's voice: 'And the doorway to the knowledge of the black man and his little song sitting at his table was the killing of a man . . .'

The hall is completely quiet again. Glass continues, in a conversational tone.

'I lived on a river-barge in those days. I had not long come from Africa. I had very little money. I had listened to the young men who had been away before me, who told me that nowadays every man should speak English, and then he could change the old ways, which had been too long in charge. I was skimping and saving and had come to England to study to learn good English.

'This barge was very cheap to rent. It was far out on the mud-flats and few people wanted to stay. The flies and the gnats bothered them, but that reminded me of home! There were immense sunsets, the great red-hot dome going down into the black river-plains streaked with those colours from the sky in their broad pools, cloud masses hanging over the gulf into which the sun was lost to view, but from which he still sent up his colours to redden those roofs, those processions like animals flowing in their many forms all day. Much of this, the Thames delta, was flooded with the rising tide twice a day, and the brackish intermingling of river and sea lifted my boat, and lapped against the sides. Then when the tide went down, water ran away in channels and streams through a re-made landscape, and I praised the moon, whose pulse also I could see alter the land, as the sun did in the seasons. Our nights and days in Equatorial Africa do not vary in length, and the spring and the autumn were new to me also, these delicate margins of process: we have only the dry and the rainy seasons. And every piece of driftwood - why, when I was homesick, which was often, I wanted every piece of driftwood or old log to open its jaws and yawn whitely with a hoarse sound like the animal that in this country you name a crocodile, but which we call by the title of "Great Mother", since she is the door to death and the ancestors, the very mouth of the river mud. Mud is full of elderspirits. We buried our dead by floating them into the river, which we know unwinds their bodies and releases their souls from that tight knot of black flesh. Our mating is therefore performed on the river mud, during the last rains, for the rain is the spirit returning, and the red mud the flesh.

'I was homesick, though I knew that new ways were coming to my country, and I was a part of those new ways, and my home would not be the same when I returned, and I would have a second tongue in my head, capable of lying for gain and not fun. I wanted to hear the river-horse ancestor and his snuffling grunt — the hippopotamus — as he rose out of the great brown river with the water streaming off his back: it is he whose swimming causes the river to flow; he is part of the grain of it, as your hearts are part of the grain of your blood-vessels. Sometimes the wind ruffled the cold waters of this chilly place to make a hump in the tide that reminded me of this god.

'Often I trudged in the dry water-meadows and watched the few young horses and remembered the gazelle-herds that would pause in their gallop and turn to look at you with a single movement, as I now stand before your gaze, Society of Glass. But at that time I had not spoken to above a dozen of English people.

'I kept my old barge warm with that driftwood that I had fancied was like crocodiles, and I learned to love the old boat though I suffered very badly from the cold at first and had to wear blankets over my shoulders and newspapers stuffed into my jacket and my shoes. The river-barge was a good home to me. With its broad brown hull and flanks and planks, dark with useful living, rich as fruit-cake, it was like a utensil my own people might have made, and it became to me like an ark full of my African memories, the firelight striped with long grass and zebra.

'My barge had one drawback. There was a landlord. He was a small farmer, called Skinner, and owned that tiny part of the Thames — as if anyone could own any part of that great grainy being — and owned some mud on which his wheat grew, and some grass on which his animals grazed, and he owned the great fallen tree that was the river-barge, and on that fallen trunk had grown a black and curious fungus: Geoffrey Glass.

'I don't suppose he had ever seen a black man before. At that time they were quite a rarity in this country of yours. He was a man who bore the world a grudge because he was childless. I think at first he had some smoky liberal idea of me as his black son, my personality fathered by his kindness, but that was all in the air and did not survive our few encounters. I came to live in his barge, and he envied my contentment, my studies, my independence, my solitary walks. He began to spy on me. I was not alarmed. My world was not broken into by watchful eyes: when the tide went down the mud became suddenly full of the all-seeing eyes of flock after flock of all kinds of birds, and their jabbing beaks; an extra human pair made no difference and perhaps that made him feel worse. I'd find him standing still in the shade of trees, and he seemed surprised that my eyes were sharp enough to make him out clearly in the twilight, to notice him hiding, and to greet him. I knew what green tussock he was behind, pretending to set an animal trap; I could see the faint prints he made with the sides of his body through the long grass up to his hiding place in the dry ditch. Then he began to carry a gun, pretending he was out to shoot duck. Occasionally after a walk I would come home and discover my things disarranged. I knew he had come into my barge while I was away, and had been sitting in my chair among my papers, watching for me out of the portholes over the flats, considering the sunset, perhaps pretending to be black like me, all dark in the shadowy hull.'

There is no tremor in the audience. Glass has been using no magic, no tricks, but each one, used to listening for the power in words, is there in the barge, as black man confronts his white shadow.

'He was not drunk that final evening. I could smell no drink. But there was a crisis in him and he was raving. I think he was always anxious and never calm. Like so many whites he hated his body, its postures, its language. It was as if it was always trying to tell him something that he would not listen to, and so he had to keep moving away from it, keep it restlessly active. He always had to be busy about something, always hurrying to and fro; even when he was shooting the birds on the mud-flats he pottered from cover to cover, and it was only when the birds were plentifully feeding on what the tide uncovered that he could splash his pools of feathers and blood on the marshes, for he was no stalker, no huntsman. I think it was only in the barge that I had made my own, in the atmosphere of living I had made within the old tree-hull, that he had been able to find peace, to sit still and feel the wood-grain in the old trunk, and the water-grain lapping at it outside.

'You may justly say that I thought smugly of myself in those days. I blasphemed; I thought — and thought sincerely, and that made it worse — that even the small gods of this world had rejected this man Skinner. I dismissed his existence with the pride of my own fullness. I thought he was in hell because he could not see the greatness of the ants, the magnificence of an eider feather, as I could. I did not know that he had in him a greater teacher than I had ever encountered.

'I knew he had come aboard when I heard him pounding three times on the deck above me with the stock of his shot-gun. There was nothing particularly abnormal in this — it was the way he knocked at my door, knocked at my deck. I called out "Come in!" and he came stumbling down the ladder. I could tell by the way he climbed down that there was something wrong. I pumped up the lamp to make the room bright and as he turned the first thing I saw was the blood on his white shirt. Then I saw the great knife in his hand.

'It was the kind I think is called a flensing knife, used for skinning animals in the tannery. I thought he had cut himself accidentally somehow in the chest and had come to me for help. I went towards him and reached and touched his flesh through the opening of his shirt. The touch of my hands on him made him jerk, and he spat out a curse and recoiled and raised the knife threateningly. His reaction — and I saw him wrinkle his nostrils too, as at the smell of that curious fungus — was to me at the time only the flinching of somebody who had been hurt, and who expected every new touch to hurt him again. So I came forward a second time. But he made a gesture with the knife as though to ward me off, and he began to shrug the jacket off that had been hung about his shoulders.

'The jacket fell to the floor. His shirt was very white. It was cut a little over his left chest, and blood was soaking it. He gripped the knife tightly in his right fist, and slowly swung the tip of it so it pointed at my eyes. Then, as deliberately, he turned it towards his own left arm and with a swift stroke cut open the sleeve-cloth and flesh. More blood leapt over the white from the long straight shallow cut through the two skins, the shirt and the skin of his body.

'Then he raised his head and looked at me directly for the first time, and grinned, showing all his teeth. Slowly, very slowly, he walked towards me, pointing at my heart with the tip of that knife. I saw that all his awkwardness had gone, and his movements since he had come down the steps had been graceful, like the movements of a hunter modelled on those of the great cat he is stalking, or like — yes, I thought this — the movements of a black man at peace with himself because he has found his purpose.

'I understood that he wanted to kill me, but had cut himself first so that he could pretend that it was self-defence; that I had attacked him and he had snatched the knife from me and used it on his attacker. I backed up the aft ladder away from him, and climbing still deliberately, still gracefully, he followed me on to the deck. There was a coil of light rope there and I was able to catch him in it like a lassoo and knock the knife out of his hands.'

The bee-hum has been growing in the hall, and though it is still very faint, it has now become a background to Glass's narrative. It circles round and round as the people utter and pass it on to the ones next to them, each one perhaps making only a very slight sound, perhaps unconsciously, something close to a deep short sigh, but in aggregate it is that hum, like a heavy insect swarming, circling the dome around the centre which is Glass; and whether the power whose audible sound increases infinitesimally each circuit is his, or the audience's, remains to be seen.

'I did not leave him and run away. No. I did not leave him tied up and go to phone for the police. No. I did with him as I wanted, which was something I had not known about myself, but which was something that I had brought to England with me.

'First I cut all his clothes off him. I had hogtied him; I had fastened his hands together with the rope and I had slipped his feet into these bonds, so that he lay on the rough planking his body strained back and his belly-skin taut. The moon was rising. He could not talk for terror. I saw his eyes, which were white, and his teeth which were white, and his face which was bone-white with fear, rolling on the dark wood of the deck. Then I did something which in my madness I called "showing the gods" to him.

'I flayed this man. I wanted to make his blood call to him, so that he would understand an intimacy with this body that he would shortly leave. I did not know that I loved him, and it was that I needed his blood to call to me. With the flensing knife he had brought, which had tasted his blood which he himself had shown to me down below, which had seen (though neither of us knew it) the token of our blood-brotherhood, I flayed him. I splashed myself and the wood on which I knelt with his offered blood. I should have slashed my own skin and mingled bloods with this man.

'I made the first cut in his stretched belly, deep through the fascia, and I reached my hands into the fatty leather and tugged, loosening its adhesions with the muscles beneath. Then I used one hand inside his skin to make a further tension, which I relieved by slipping the knife into it and expanding the slit upwards to his throat. After one long, bubbling cry he was silent, though his ribs, creamy like long piano keys, still heaved.

'Then I performed the same action along his arms and his legs, and peeled the skin off like bark from a sapling. Some of the hot blood was congealing, and in the moonlight it was like working with my hands in thick molasses. I then dissected the genitals out with the small reverse blade of the knife, which was designed for this purpose, and from the throat dissected the mask off the true face which grinned up at me from its lidless eyes. With a heave, I turned that face away, and pulled the entire skin off the back, grasping the skin of the throat from behind, and pulling backwards off the skull and shoulders. I had to incise at wrists and ankles, leaving the skin clothing the hands and feet like gloves and socks of white, because I did not want to loosen or release the bonds in case he came to and, in the agony of his skinlessness, struggled or convulsed. But he was passive.

'I took the skin off him like a heavy drenched suit, lined with wet plush. I piled it in a heap to one side, in the scuppers, where it continued to bleed. I turned my carcass over and smiled back at its smile. I told him he knew something of life now, and I would teach him something about water. He would be joined to the river by the graft of his skinless body, and the whole river would be his new, reflecting skin. "But you will not want these clothes," I said. I heaved the loose skin over the side, and watched it swirl like a ghost down through the current. I threw his ordinary clothes after it, and they floated for a bit, then sank. Then I took my old friend who grinned up at me, over my shoulder and jumped into the water with him.

'I had tied one end of a long rope to a cleat on one side of the deck, and took that down with us. In the water I could not at first see anything at all for the cloud of blood, but the moonlight was strong, and I soon glimpsed his lipless smile through the water. I dived — we were wrapped together like lovers swimming — and took him with me under the hull of the barge, which had about six feet of clearance from the oozy bottom. My lungs were good for this task, and without difficulty I laid him directly under the ridge of the hull, which loomed above us. Here I took up the slack of the rope and fastened it to the knot I had made with his hands tied together with his feet. Then I took the loose rope in my hand and soared up through the water, breaking into the moonlight on the other side of the boat.

'I reasoned that if he were under the hull of the boat, it would not be long before a few tides, pressing the whole weight of the barge on him, ground him to bits. I thought the skin was light enough to be carried away on the tide, and I enjoyed the sardonic jest of letting a white man's whiteness be carried away on the black water, while his essential red part remained behind him, to be pressed out like grapes below my home. As for myself, I was clean by passing through the waters. I pulled the other end of his rope taut and fastened it to the corresponding cleat on the other side of the deck. Then I went below and slept very well indeed.

'In the morning my madness and my triumph was still with me. I exulted. I went up on deck and looked across the marshes. The tide was down and the mud was alive with birds. Far out on a mudbank I saw a particular concentration of feathers and tugging movements, and this concentration was sprawled out in the shape of a man, flickering with the wings of birds like white fire. I gasped as I realised that the skin had been cast up on this bank. I hoped the birds would eat it or carry it away before anyone found this shell of the man I had killed. As I hoped this, a small rowing-boat carrying several men rounded the point into view,

'Not long afterwards the police were on my deck asking me questions. I said I knew nothing, while two launches passed down the channel carrying a dragnet between them, troubling the reflections of the water that was usually so calm during the earliest part of the morning. Each wavelet that passed over the water was as though a skin was being taken from my body. I lied, but the lies were like skins that the ripples were taking away. Frogmen clumped on to the deck, and with awkward splashes made many more ripples that peeled away over the waters, troubling the lies that I had created, the images of myself that I wished to reflect to the inspector who questioned me. Some of his colleagues hauled a wet frogman on to the deck. He slipped his glass mask on to the crown of his head and without a word and with great flopping footprints walked over to one of those cleats and unfastened the rope. He threw it into the water, and motioned to his colleagues to help him on the other side. Without a further word they drew on the rope.

'At the trial my lies were repeated, and as they told them over to me I unpeeled them and told the truth. They told me that I should have pleaded guilty but insane, but I wanted the image of my innocence to be built up in court, so that it could be slowly unpeeled of all its falsehoods. At the end, when I stood before the judge to be sentenced, I felt myself to be one great seeing unlidded skinless eye as I faced the staring eye of the judge.'

Glass's voice changes and the rapping of the gavel proceeds from his mouth and the sounds of a courtroom scene also, and the sniffly penetrating voice of the judge: 'A DELIBERATE SAVAGE MURDER. HAVE YOU ANYTHING TO SAY BEFORE SENTENCE IS PASSED?'

'As I looked at him the judge in his judging robes changed into the dead man. His robes of red and white had become the robes and representation of a carcass, like the mask of a god in a dance. I saw the judge in his red and white and black like the dead man I had created, mistaking love for death. I thought I had brought him to life with exquisite agony and punished him when

I removed that misleading skin coloured like lard to show him what we all had in common, but I was showing myself myself, and stealing his death for my own education. That education now proceeded. I knew I would not now be able to see anything but that red and that white and that black and that this was my torment and I was in hell.'

The words 'in hell' softly hum round and round the dome of the seated multitude.

'And I sat alone with my judge.'

'My judge' is uttered softly in humming syllables by the multitude.

'He and I SATATASATATASATATASATATATABLESATATA TABLESATATAT ABLE together, me on one side of the wood and he on the other like endless reflecting reality, he staring and grinning at me and I staring and grinning at him, the two of us reflecting over and over like parallel mirrors down and down into the grain of reality until the reality of what I had done had soaked so deeply within me that I could grip it like a door and swing it aside. And over that threshold I learnt — *I heard — the lesson that I had given — had thought to give — the dead man so quickly; I learnt between the black and the white the song of the red blood, like bees building their hive . . .'*

'Their hive' comes winging from the lips of the multitude that faces him across the table.

'I myself became the dead man, and I knocked on the deck SATATASATATASATATA and my black pupil invited me in and I descended and he dressed me in my scarlet and creamy robes, and I imprisoned him, and sat with him in his prison until he had delivered me from my skin that had imprisoned me. A prison was I to him who imprisoned me.'

A prison was I . . .
'A mirror was I to him who reflected me . . .
A mirror was I.
'I was wounded and I shall wound.'
I was wounded and I shall wound.
'A doorway am I to him who knocks . . .
A doorway are we to them who knock.

'I will be saved and I will save.'
We shall be saved and we will save . . .

Each syllable is passed round the great hall, round and round until it vibrates and merges into the hum which is uttering these words, or the words that are creating the hum. At first Glass speaks, and the multitude speaks after him in response, but soon he and they are speaking together and the great spinning echoes of the hall are, as it were, catching up with each other so that the force of the bee-hum increases with each sentence uttered, and at last there is only the meaning, and the vibration that is in that meaning.

'I will be saved and I will save
I will be freed and I will free
I will be wounded and I will wound
I will be begotten and I will beget
I will hear and I will be heard
I will be known, who am spirit
A mirror are we to thee who discernest me
A door are we to thee who knockest at me
A way are we to thee who passest

Thou hearest that I suffered, but I suffered not
Blood flowed from me and yet did not flow
To each and all I proclaim the end of madness
To each and all it is given to dance
We give thanks to darkness in which there is light
We give thanks to the light in which there is darkness
I will hear and I will be heard
I will be wounded and I will wound
I will be freed and I will free
I will consume and I will be consumed
I will know and I will be known
I will mourn: mourn all
I will rejoice: rejoice all
I will flee and I will stay
He who joins not in the dance mistakes the event

I will adorn and I will be adorned
I will enter and I will be entered
I will change and I will be changed
A body have I not and bodies have I
A glass am I to thee who perceivest me
A door am I to thee who knockest at me
A way am I to thee who passest . . .'

'We can't have this,' said the sardonic bishop, leaning across the row to Canon John, shouting to make himself heard.

'No, we can't,' said John decidedly.

'Come on then,' said the sardonic one. And they struggled out of the front row past the rapt people, who did not notice them going.

'Wait, I'm coming too,' said the wool-haired bishop, who had been sitting with his friend.

'Where are we going?' asked John, as they dived into one of the sloping aisles that led beneath the stage.

'Look!' said the sardonic bishop, unlocking a door and gesturing at the humming transformers and mains switches that were below the stage; 'I know how to stop their nonsense.' In the corridor outside, lights streamed down from the hail, and the words of the sayings spoken out of the humming, so slowly accelerating and gathering, came down to them. 'I'll pull their plugs, I'll blow their fuses,' said the sardonic one, grasping an immense switch. The wool-headed bishop was at the doorway, not paying much attention to his friends, but listening dreamily to the sounds from the hall, white head cocked to one side. 'Singing masons building roofs of gold. . .'

'What's that, Cedric, scripture again?' said the sardonic bishop, pausing at the switch.

'Shakespeare, actually, Henry V, Act V,' said Cedric.

'I'll Shakespeare *them,'* said the bishop pulling down the switch and plunging the room into darkness. But light still streamed down the corridor from the hall, and showed each the others' white faces.

'What is it?' whispered John, as they crept back.

'The hall is still full of light, even though there is no electricity.

It is brighter than sunshine,' said the sardonic one. Cedric looked back at them.

'A feasting presence, full of light,' he said from the threshold; 'Romeo and Juliet, Act V, Scene III.'

All three came out into the body of the hall, John puffing with the weight of his belly in which the baby had been quiet for some days now. The rows of chairs in the arena, the soaring galleries and valances, the balconies hanging like branches full of glowing fruit on the inside of the great sphere, were packed with dazzling light, and the three men hid their faces in their hands. Soon, by dint of peeping between their fingers, they could see more clearly that this light was pouring from the bodies of the multitude, from its flesh. The faces were dazzling, but in the bright faces the mouths gave forth brighter rays that were words, that were at the same time radiation of light and the deep humming that now seemed so profound that it might have been the sound of the earth sipping the nectar of space as it span on its orbit. The clothes of the people hung on their bodies like filmy woven shadows. Glass stood behind his table on the white-draped platform, but now there was a change, as though his flesh were radiating *black* light, for the drapery that had been so snowy was a pulsating luminous black, and Geoffrey Glass's clothes were fluorescing sheer white. The table in front of him was a table of solid light in which a mass of woven flames flowed compactly in the patterns of the grain of wood or of a river of white fire, but the table was not consumed. Then Glass raised his head that was haloed with hair shining white, in which a deep blackness uttered light that sprang from his lips into the great light of his multitude. The note of the hum changed, and seemed to convey a greater serenity. Much of the light in the hall now began to take shape within the bodies, like a heavy liquid; like shining mercury it dropped downwards and gathered beneath the waistlines of the garments, but so bright was it that the brightness of the hall was in no way diminished. The deeper hum continued; it was as if serenity unfolded upon serenity. All three clergymen now took their hands away from their eyes as they stood with their backs to the underworld beneath the stage, amazed at the flowering tree of light that was unfolding beneath this roof. Their hands clasped into the natural attitude of prayer. Their bodies felt full of energy and calm, like flowers expanding in the summer sunshine, in the magnetism of a good season. The sardonic one's cheeks were wet with tears; the wool-headed bishop's eyes were nearly starting out of his head and his smile threatened to split his old face in two.

Then the hall screamed!

At the same time John felt a racking of pain in his body that threw him on to his knees. Another great scream resounded and bounded like light in mirrors from round wall to round wall. The light from the bodies suddenly went out and there was a blackness all the more total for the light that had gone before. 'What has gone wrong, what could have gone wrong?' was as much as John could say out of his spiritual and bodily agony as the dreadful cramping pains drove into him and jerked him into a sitting position with his head as near to his knees as his great hard belly would allow. Then with a drench of paler, poorer light, the hall's electric lights came on, and under them John could see the chaos of people, some hurrying to and from the doors, very many like himself on the floor with people bending over them. He saw white-coated figures with emergency medical bags hurrying through the aisles and stopping near the recumbent figures. He felt hands take his own head and gently lay it on a pillow, and spread a foamrubber mattress under him, and a sheet on top of that. He found himself turned over and the clothes lifted from his back, and something cold swabbed there, and a small needle-prick and a numbness spreading. Then he felt the greater needle go into his back to block the nerves in his spine so that he could have his baby without the general anaesthetic that would make him unconscious. As they were turning him back, he saw a woman nearby. She was sitting on an ordinary chair, and smiling with concentrated pleasure as the contractions took hold. The people around her were laughing with pleasure. A woman bent forward and said to her with joy, 'Your baby's nearly here!'

John looked from his pillow at his mountainous tummy, that was visibly clenching inside, though he felt nothing. The skin was stretched and the abdomen pushed forward exactly as he had visualised Glass's victim, tied hand and foot, ready for the flaying. John knew what was coming, and mentally gave himself to the knife as the skin was swabbed and the surgeon bent over him. As the silver blade bit deeply, blood splashed across the front of the white overalls.

The knife glided through the first incision, and the surgeon spread the flaps in an almond-shaped aperture. John heard a joyful shout from the mother and the women nearby; he thought this must be happening all round the world, and their time would have come for everyone, and the radio broadcast too would have triggered the new babies into the world; he realised that when the hall screamed it had been the scream of pain and outrage from the men, and not the women. His surgeon now made a second cut into John's belly, crosswise to the first, and probed with his glove-covered finger. A nurse held a retractor, to keep the flaps well spread. Then forceps were passed in, and clipped at either end for a third cut, longitudinal again, that would go directly into John's male womb and expose the baby's head. The surgeon took a long tonsil-knife and made this cut slowly and carefully, tucked his hand deep into the wound, and slid the child's face to the front with his finger in its mouth. John saw the face of his child, bright red, snooded in the wrappings of his three wounds, frowning, the eyes tightly closed. Then it was like a flower opening and the child at the centre of it growing out as the surgeon scooped and put the baby into John's arms, and opened the front of his cassock where his great male nipples had grown hard and erect. John saw the looping ropes of the umbilicus trailing from his inside, and the surgeon waiting with clamps. The baby sneezed all over John's chest, took in a great breath and gave a sigh, and the surgeon clamped the cord in two places, cutting between them, for the child no longer needed to breathe through his father's blood. John did not see this, for with a sudden instinct he put his daughter to his breast, and he felt the strong gums rubbing at his nipple like a cat lapping. Thrills of pleasure and love went through his body, and he wished the epidural anaesthetic had not been necessary, and that he could have felt more, even the knife cutting into him. The baby stopped sucking and pulled away from his nipple, and John immediately felt deep concern. He looked down into the child's face, and as he did so the soft, toothless mouth writhed sweetly, and the eyes opened and smiled straight into his eyes.

'I love you, Father,' lisped the new-born child.

Round the whole hall he hears the new babies declaring their love, and their tiny voices merge into a hum like the sound of the earth itself, spinning on its true orbit.

Author's Note

The God of Glass is a fictional rehearsal of themes that were later treated factually with full documentation in *The Wise Wound* by Penelope Shuttle and Peter Redgrove (London, Gollancz; New York, Marek: 1978). These themes include the origin of witchcraft in the subjective experience of the human fertility cycle *(The Wise Wound,* Chapter VI); the healing of madness by shamanistic practices through the mediation of the 'devil', *animus,* or 'other husband' of the woman (Chapter III); and the emergence of these preoccupations in present-day horror films and novels of exorcism (Chapter VII). Mr Glass's magic ballad is discussed on pages 211ff. of *The Wise Wound;* the act of flaying on page 139; and the hosts of animals on pages 122ff. The apparent violence of certain of the scenes is the natural accompaniment to the emergence of deeply repressed but healing material. *The God of Glass is* subtitled 'A Morality' because it seeks, by adopting the mode and idiom of a horror story of exorcism, to redirect attention to the serious themes of adult rebirth, and the dire consequences of masculine non-participation in feminine blood-mysteries, behind the usually conventionalised currency of the modern supernatural tale. Mr Glass is a black man because the author considers that the black African races are more knowledgeable concerning healing shamanistic practices than are, at present, the European peoples.

www.ingramcontent.com/pod-product-compliance
Lightning Source LLC
LaVergne TN
LVHW091008080826
845145LV00003B/1184